SEED SAVERS
lily

DON'T MISS BOOK ONE OF THE
SEED SAVERS SERIES:
TREASURE

They say you should remember the past...But sometimes you need to remember the future.

Clare, Dante, and Lily live in a future where growing vegetables is against the law. Some, however, encourage the children to change the future, and instruct them in the old ways.

Can the children learn enough before being stopped by GRIM, the government agency controlling the nation's food?

And can children really change the future?

SEED SAVERS
lily

S. Smith

SEED SAVERS
BOOK TWO: LILY

ISBN-13: 978-0615720296
ISBN-10: 0615720293

This is a work of fiction. Names, characters, businesses, places, events and incidents are either the products of the author's imagination or used in a fictitious manner. Any resemblance to actual persons, living or dead, or actual events is purely coincidental.

Cover design and image by Aileen Smith Photography.

seedsaversseries.com

*For Moe Parr, Percy Schmeiser, Vernon Bowman,
and all the others whose lives have been turned
upside down because they saved seeds.*

When I let go of what I am,
I become what I might be.
Lao Tzu

chapter 1

MY NAME IS LILY. When I first heard Clare and Dante were missing and presumed runaway, I couldn't believe it. Clare is my best friend, after all, and her brother Dante like the brother I never had. Hadn't I just seen them? Didn't I see them practically every day of my life? They weren't the kind of kids who run away.

But when I learned the rest of the story, the pieces started falling into place. Clare's mom had been arrested on charges of illegal plant possession. It was only one plant—a tomato—but it was highly illegal. And I knew something the local cops didn't know. I knew the plant belonged to Clare, Dante, and me. I knew we were the ones involved in the unlawful activities of seed saving and growing food. I knew our friend Ana, the senior citizen who was our mentor, had recently disappeared. A simple runaway case? Definitely not. Clare and Dante ran to save their mother. They ran to save the seeds. They ran to save the future and the present, and something of the past.

It was my mom who first told me about Clare and Dante's disappearance. Actually, it was more like an interrogation, only gentler, because it was Ma. She asked me all sorts of questions, starting with *when did you last see either of them* and ending with *no one had seen the siblings in twenty-four hours*. Apparently the cops had visited our place having heard Clare and I were friends; the homes of all classmates and friends had been checked on the chance the children may have slept over without telling their mom. That's the story the cops gave Ma, anyway. As I would find out later, they themselves had jailed Mrs. James earlier that day. All Ma knew was that my best friends in the whole world were missing, and she wanted to make sure I wasn't harboring important information as to their whereabouts. The police assured her it looked like a runaway case rather than an abduction (bikes and backpacks were gone) so at least she wasn't freaking out that I might get kidnapped.

The fact was, I hadn't seen Clare and Dante since Sunday. Being summer break, there wasn't the daily interaction of school, and they were attending tech day camp, so we weren't together as much as usual. After Ma questioned me, I tried to remember our last conversations; were Clare and Dante having family trouble that would cause them to leave home? I couldn't believe they would ever act so drastically. And I would know if something was up. My only conclusion was that they were forced to leave, or left in a hurry unable to tell me.

As soon as I got the chance, I rode my bike over to their apartment. Yellow police tape surrounded the cement stoop where we had often sat talking and conspiring. The door to their flat was wide open. So empty. I wondered where their mother was.

Something's not right, I said to myself. Reflexively, I rode out of sight and watched from across the street behind a parked truck. And then I saw *him* with the local police, a man from GRIM: the Green Resource Investigation Machine. A federal enforcer of all things plant and food related.

I sped home and raced to my room, closing the door behind me and locking it. I was out of breath, but not from the physical exertion. In one of my last conversations with Clare, she had shared her fears that something had happened to our friend and mentor, Ana. Ana had not been to church—the only place the two of them felt safe meeting—and it had worried Clare. I had told her to calm down, that she was over-reacting.

And now Clare and Dante were gone, too.

Think, I told myself. *What would Clare and Dante do?* I figured they'd pray, for one, but I didn't really know much about that. In our apartment we had a little altar which currently held a couple of Carbo squares and flowers. Ma set out something new most days. One time, when I had woken up early, I found her standing silently in front of it, holding in her hands little paper strips dotted with Japanese characters. I had quietly watched but decided against asking her about it. I think that may have been prayer. I didn't know if Clare and Dante's God was among the collection of gods my mom prayed to or not. Clare's way of praying resembled talking to God as if he were a person in the room listening, as if he would get back to you. I figured a Bible might help, considering Ana had used a Bible a lot in class, but we didn't own one.

I decided to keep a low profile; maybe Clare and Dante were hiding somewhere for a reason I had yet to discover. What didn't make sense to me was that it had looked like *nobody* was home; where was Clare's mom? Either way, I didn't like the way people seemed to be disappearing. I stayed home the next day. Ma appreciated the extra help folding the tiny paper cranes she sold for income in gift stores and craft bazaars.

On Friday I rode over to Clare's place again. By then the yellow tape was gone, as were the cops. I saw a light on in the house. I rode up and pulled my bicycle around the back. I couldn't help gazing toward the place our carrots had been fiercely growing, like the outlaws they were. Gone! The ground torn up without a trace of the carrots we'd lovingly and patiently tended. I sidled up the stairs and knocked.

The door opened. Clare's mom stood there, looking more harried and haggard than ever. Dark circles hung under her eyes like rain clouds in the late autumn sky. I could tell she hadn't slept and had probably done a lot of crying.

"Lily!"

She reached out to hug me. It was as if she'd forgotten about me until that moment. I don't know what came over me. Frankly, I was relieved to find her there, but for whatever reason, and totally beyond my will to do so, tears welled up. We held each other crying there in the doorway for several minutes. Then she let go and ushered me in, telling me to sit.

That was when I found out about her arrest for the tomato plant.

"I spoke to Clare on the phone," she told me over and over. "But they held me for two more days. When I called the second day, no one answered. Those damned policemen wouldn't let me call again, and they told me not to worry. I knew something was wrong."

I listened quietly.

"Lily," she said, "where are my children?"

I didn't know what to do. I knew a lot more than she did, but Clare had always felt the less her mother knew, the better off she would be in a situation such as this.

"I don't know," I answered truthfully. "I heard the police think they left on their own." The words "ran away" seemed harsh to say aloud.

"Yes," she admitted. "Both backpacks, bikes, a flashlight, food—all gone. It definitely does not look like a kidnapping."

We sat, silent. At last I said, "They're together. Clare will take good care of Dante."

She clasped my hand and smiled just a bit, her cheeks glistening with tears.

"Thanks for that, Lily," she whispered. "But why? Why did they go?" Her dark and hollowed eyes bored into me.

I shrugged my shoulders. I had a pretty good idea it had something to do with GRIM and the seized plant, but my head was still spinning with my own selfish question: *Why didn't they take me?*

chapter 2

SO THERE I WAS, mid-summer and suddenly my best friends had disappeared. The only thing that kept me going was tending the vegetables I'd planted around town. You can say I'm a bad friend if you want, but I couldn't wait for next year. Clare had entrusted me with the bulk of Ana's seeds, and I'd chosen to go ahead and plant some this season. She hadn't been in favor of planting in vacant lots or roadsides around town when I'd floated the idea; she wanted us to start more slowly. I couldn't wait; I snuck out and planted anyway. And my seeds had prospered. I had fine-looking plants hidden all over the neighborhood. I knew I'd tell her sooner or later.

Visiting my plants was good therapy as I tried to figure out why Clare and Dante ran, why they didn't tell me, and where they might be headed.

But as inspirational as the crunchy red radishes were, I couldn't come up with any answers. From what I knew of my friend, I figured she ran away to protect her mother, and she *didn't* run here, to protect me. Or maybe she thought GRIM would stop us, so she ran to continue the Movement— this seemed to me a very brave thing for a thirteen-year-old. But where she ran to, I didn't have a clue.

The more I thought about it, though, the only answer I could come up with was that she had tried to find Ana's house. I, too, had a map to Ana's. But what if all of them had been caught by GRIM, and GRIM only made it look like they were runaways? Would I be the next to disappear? A chill ran down my spine as I imagined my mother at the kitchen table, folding her origami alone.

I couldn't stand it any longer. In my daily rides around town, spying my secret gardens, I never saw evidence of GRIM agents tailing me. I knew I must try to find Ana's house.

That evening, after sufficient small talk with Ma, I excused myself to my room. I dug out the map Ana had given us in case of emergency and carefully studied the route to her house. I guessed it might take half an hour by bike. I needed a plan.

I arose early the next morning and left a note on the table for Ma. I apologized for not asking permission and told her I would be out all day with the family of a friend from school—told her I was lonely without Clare. Part of it was true, anyway. I assured her the whole family would be along since she liked knowing who I was with. I even threw in a name, to make it seem more real: *My friend, Rose*, I wrote. I loaded my backpack with emergency supplies should anything go wrong: food, juice, a jacket; and stuffed all the small change I could find into my pockets. I applied sunscreen carefully, put on a micro-helmet topped with a wide-brimmed hat my mother had woven just for me, tucked sunglasses in a pocket, then rode off into the burgeoning dawn.

Not many people were out and the joggers I passed mostly ignored me. The ride was pleasant and I was thankful for the minor amount of insects vying to fly into my mouth and nose. I gave up trying to play out in my mind what would happen once I found Ana's place. There were just too many unknowns. Instead, I focused on the words of a favorite song, singing it over and over in my head as my legs pushed the pedals round and round.

It took longer than I had guessed to reach Ana's house, but as I drew nearer the matching street number, there was no doubt which one it was. Over the summer we had learned quite a lot about food-bearing plants, and I recognized in Ana's landscaping certain edible specimens. The flowers—reds, yellows, oranges—tiered in height from groundcover to five feet tall, were a rare treat. A sweet fragrance hung over the place like a jungle canopy. Ana's small yard was more beautiful than any park I'd ever experienced. I guess I'm not sure what I was expecting, but I think I had in mind a crime scene, like at Clare's. A dug-up yard, boarded windows, yellow tape. A look of vacancy. After all, it had been a few weeks since Ana supposedly had gone missing. But this place flourished.

I jumped off my bike and walked it up the stone-scattered driveway, glancing around nervously. Why did I suddenly feel like Hansel and Gretel reaching for the shingles on the candy house? I rapped tentatively on the front door, and then seeing the button, rang the doorbell. I waited a few moments and was about to turn away when I heard a familiar voice call out.

"Yes, yes, I'm coming, I'm coming."

The door opened and there she stood. Ana.

"Lily?"

The look of amazement on her face was startling, but so must have been the same on mine.

"Ana?"

We stood dumb, staring. Finally Ana moved. She stepped out of the doorway, peering around.

"Is it just you?" she asked. "Where are Clare and Dante? Why, I can't believe it," she said. "It's so good to see you. But—"

The stipulations Ana had given us about using the map to find her home were clear: Don't—unless something happens.

"—What's happened, Lily?"

She pulled me into her house.

"Please, sit down."

I sat. She looked at me, waiting for an answer, for an explanation as to my presence here. I was temporarily dumbstruck; still in a daze at finding Ana here, alive and well, everything normal. Ana —in front of me in her cute little house—not missing at all.

"Lily," she repeated, "what's wrong?"

It was only then I noticed how much thinner she looked, that she used a cane as she crossed the room. A walker stood in the corner.

"I, I didn't think I'd find you here." Even as I spoke, my mind raced, trying to fit the new information into place, bits and pieces, past and present. Maybe she'd seen Clare and Dante, maybe everything was fine.

"Clare was worried when you missed church," I heard my words, as if someone else was speaking. In the conversation running just ahead in my imagination Ana was laughing and saying, *Oh yes, I know, she and Dante told me, after the GRIM agents raided their home. We thought it better for them to stay here for awhile. But things have calmed down, that's why they rode into town today to get you. Where did you say they are now?*

"Lily? Lily—are you okay?" Ana's real voice broke through the imagined one I'd been listening to.

"Did you hear me, child?"

"No, sorry," I mumbled. "I was thinking about something else."

"I must get you something to drink," she said, grasping her cane to pull herself up.

"Oh, no," I replied, jumping up. "You stay, I can help myself."

I scrambled to the kitchen, glad to get away to collect myself. I surveyed my surroundings: a black and white checkered kitchen table with four matching chairs in front of a larger than ordinary stove; a refrigerator, the hum of which indicated it was still used to keep things cold; white cupboards lining the walls on either side of a large double sink; and a shiny black counter dotted with an array of glass jars and wooden boxes.

"The cupboard to the right of the sink," she called out.

"Thanks."

I filled my glass from the tap, urging myself to calm down. I drank slowly, then returned to the living room.

"Very well, Lily, where do we need to start?"

"Clare and Dante are gone," I burst. "No one knows where they are!"

chapter 3

"CLARE AND DANTE ARE MISSING?"

"Yes." I stifled the would-be sobs into a few sniffles. "They ran away after the police and GRIM agents raided their apartment and put their mom in jail. I've only just been trying to figure everything out. Ana, haven't you heard about it on the Monitor?" I glanced around the tidy living room. Unlike most places, with a Monitor as large as a window prominently displayed, this room was oddly devoid of one.

"As you can see, my dear, I don't own a Monitor. I occasionally use one when I'm in town, at the library or the senior center. Sometimes even at plug-in stations. I prefer not to have one in my home so that it doesn't come to own me. I know too many people who have stopped living their lives and do everything virtually. Keeping the Monitor out of my home works for me. But tell me, what happened?"

"They accused Clare and Dante's mom, Celia, of growing illegal plants. They took our tomato and pulled up the carrots. But they never found any seeds or other things to implicate her as a Seed Saver and she kept denying everything, so they let her go. But Clare and Dante were gone by then. You haven't heard from them?"

She shook her gray head.

"Where were you, Ana? Why weren't you in church? Clare was worried that GRIM got you."

She nodded her head toward the walker. "I fell and broke my hip. I was in the care center for a time. I thought Clare would hear about it that first week in church."

"She missed a Sunday," I murmured.

Ana looked at me with a fear, or maybe sadness, that I'd never seen in her.

"Do you think that's part of the reason they ran?" she asked.

I know I should have comforted her and said no.

"I don't know. But, yeah, maybe," I answered honestly. It hurt her, me telling her she was responsible. The long-haired cat nestled in her lap sensed it, and accused me with its golden eyes.

"Oh, dear," Ana said. "How long have they been gone? You must tell me everything."

I filled her in with what I knew. Oddly, she was extremely concerned about *me*. Did I see GRIM agents following me, she wanted to know. Did the police question me? What did the police say to my mother? I assured her that I wasn't the one in trouble and suggested we focus on Clare and Dante.

"Clare's mom doesn't have any idea why they ran away," I added. "She's really sad. She looks terrible. Should I tell her what I know?"

Ana didn't answer right away. I knew she was thinking it over. At last she spoke.

"What do you think, Lily? Can she handle it? Would she be supportive enough of the Movement not to jeopardize it?"

I felt a shift of power, then, that made my stomach twinge. I was being asked my twelve-year-old (almost thirteen) opinion on whether or not I thought an *adult* could be trusted with important information. I thought about Celia—how she sometimes preferred to be kept in the dark about things. And I thought of my mother and how lost she would be if anything happened to me. Then I remembered Celia's attitude toward the authorities, and the story Clare had told us about her mom facing down the GRIM agents.

"Yes, Ana. She can be trusted," I said. "Celia wouldn't rat us out. It might be hard to keep her in one place if she thought she knew where they went. But I believe if we tell her everything, she won't let us down."

"Okay," Ana said. "In my experience, that has not always been the case. Seed Savers must be people with strong spirits. I trust your judgment. You may tell her about what's been happening. But give out as little information as possible. She needn't know my name."

With that, Ana had asked one more thing of me. She gave me instructions on how to send a coded alert about Clare and Dante out on the Network. I was to use a Monitor in a public location and make sure no one was watching. Afterwards, I had to burn the small piece of paper with the instructions and code. It was a limited one-way interaction.

Before the sun set, I had accomplished my mission.

chapter 4

I DIDN'T GET INTO TOO MUCH trouble with my mom for leaving like I did. But it caused a rather awkward situation. Ma insisted on meeting Rose and her family. I only knew one person named Rose. I had met her at the after-school tutoring session earlier in the year. We weren't exactly friends, but I figured if I could find her around town she would be more than willing to hang out —she was that sort of kid—a regular third wheel. Why her name had popped into my head the morning I left the note, I have no idea. But my fate was sealed. Once my mother got an idea in her head there was no stopping her. I would have to find Rose and get chummy fast.

It was supposed to be hot all week, so I got up early to ride around town while the weather was decent. I ached to water my outlaw veggies, but hoped instead for Mother Nature to take care of them. I kept my eyes open for any sign of Rose. How on earth was I going to find her?

Back at the apartment I ate lunch with Ma—a tray of the usual balanced food: Vitees, Proteins, and Carbos. I'm not sure why she made me sit at a table to eat with her—it's not like anyone ever sat together to eat meals anymore; most kids ate while working at or watching the Monitor. Sometimes Ma could be so old-fashioned. I often wondered what she would think of the whole "plant seeds/grow your own food" thing with which I was involved. But I remembered Ana's words—you had to be strong. Somehow this didn't seem like my mom. I always thought of her as the more fragile type.

So there we were, eating our packets together; less than a day had passed and already she was hinting about meeting Rose again.

"Ma, Rose and her family went away for a few days," I answered.

"Oh, that's too bad. At least they invited you for their day trip."

"Yes, Ma," I squashed the urge to roll my eyes.

She smiled at me politely. What was it about Asians that made them so polite? It sure hadn't rubbed off on me. Then again, maybe I just took after my pop.

I never knew my dad, and my mom didn't speak about him. When I was little I told everyone I didn't have a father. Eventually I discovered it wasn't biologically possible. But when I dared ask Ma about it all she said was, "Lily, your father is no longer with us. Do not speak it again." She was so serious and so pained-looking that I'd only ever mentioned it twice. I figured he must have died a terribly tragic death. In the story I imagined, my parents had a wild and romantic courtship and loved each other deeply. I was the sole product of that love before my dad was tragically and ruthlessly taken from us. My mother remained heartbroken, and thus, could never talk to me about him. James David Gardener. That's all I knew about him. I loved him immensely.

The too-hot afternoons dragged by without Clare and Dante.

"I'm going to the fountain in the park," I told my mom. "Maybe I can cool off."

"Be careful."

"You be careful yourself," I teased. She smiled sheepishly and waved me off.

The park was awash in people—all crowded together in one of two places: the shade of the grand maples or splashing in the fountain. The city had closed its last public pool years before I was born—budget cuts—and never reopened it. The fountains around town were the best most folks could do on scorchers like today. Sometimes I even figured it was a miracle they kept those open; of course they only had to operate them a few months out of the year—perhaps the saving grace.

I kept my distance at first, under the trees, just nabbing a touch of shade. But the water teased me like an advertisement. Not one to hold back, I finally let my bike lie, kicked off my flip flops, and rushed into the crowd. The water was cold, but cold was what I needed. I closed my eyes and bent my head back, letting the spray from the fountain pound my upturned face. That's when I heard it—the overly-loud voice which had often annoyed me at tutoring earlier in the year—the voice of red-haired Rose.

I opened my eyes and scanned the area. Sure enough, there she was, bossing around three younger kids like she owned the place. What luck! I'd found her without even trying. And by the looks of her company, she would probably jump at the chance to spend time with me. I edged my way through the throng, wondering if she'd remember me, and figuring out just what I'd say to her. I needn't have worried. While I was yet fifteen feet away, Rose whipped around, intent on chastising one of her little friends, or charges—I wasn't sure which—when her eyes glanced over me and then ricocheted back.

"Hey," she called, "what's up?"

I turned and looked behind me.

"I'm talkin' to you."

I smiled weakly. "Oh, uh, nothin'."

Rose abandoned the small children and was standing next to me in a flash.

"What about them?" I asked.

"Just kids; don't really know 'em. What's yer name ... Lavender?"

"Lily," I said.

"Yeah—I knew it was a flower—like me."

She smiled then, and for the first time it occurred to me that Rose was sort of pretty. Her red hair was overly fluffy and wild, but her features were really rather nice, a fine small nose and bright green eyes with gold flecks. Creamy skin with just enough freckles to be interesting. The smile helped me see what her previous scowls had always hidden, the way sunshine illuminates a snow-covered mountain from out of the shadows.

"Right," I said. "You're Rose."

She was pleased and impressed that I remembered her name. We ran around and splashed until we were soaked. Rose was a lot more fun than I'd anticipated. Asking her back to my place would be easy.

"Can you come over to my apartment?" I asked as we sat on the edge of the fountain, flapping our feet up and down in the water.

"Now?"

"Yeah, sure, why not?"

"Where do you live?"

"Ferndale Apartments."

"Off Dixon?"

"Yeah."

"You on your bike?"

"Yeah, it's over there," I said, motioning to where it lay near the tree. Several other bikes were piled next to it.

"Good. Me, too. Let's ride around 'til we're dry. Your folks home?"

"My mom."

Oh shoot. It dawned on me that my mom might mention to Rose how nice it was that her family had taken me vacationing with them. Not to mention that I'd just told her Rose and her family were out of town.

"Oh, no," I said dramatically.

"What?"

"I just remembered my mom isn't feeling well. I'm sorry, Rose. I can't have you over after all."

"That's okay. No biggie."

We sat splashing our feet for a few more moments.

"Lily?"

"Yes?"

"I heard about your friends."

I didn't say anything.

"Have you found out anything new? Like, does anyone know what happened to them?"

"No."

"I guess you must miss her—"

"—and Dante," I added vehemently. "Dante's gone too."

"Yeah, sure."

I didn't want to talk about it. I barely knew Rose. All I'd been thinking of in every spare moment was Clare and Dante and where they might be and whether or not they were all right. I certainly didn't need snoopy old Rose bringing it up when I had actually ceased dwelling on it for two seconds.

My terse mention of Dante and the ensuing silence had the desired effect; she dropped the subject. Suddenly Rose launched like a rocket from her seat and ran head-on into the fray, screaming as she ran. She certainly had an energy that was new to me. I wondered then and there if this might be the beginning of a strange new friendship.

chapter 5

WHEN I FIGURED MA might be worried, I headed home. I played some Monitor games and we watched a few shows together. The apartment was steamy hot, even with the fans. Finally it grew late enough to leave Ma and go to my room. There were so many things I needed to think about, plan for.

I would make a list. It always helped me to write things down. After all, the reason I had vegetables planted all over town was because I'd first drawn it all out on paper. To put ink to paper was somehow to begin. And yet it bothered my ma that I wrote. "Is that schoolwork?" she'd ask if she saw me writing. If I said no, she scowled or even chastised me. "Why you alway writing? Too much writing not so good." I didn't argue. I just learned to do it alone in my room, or off outside somewhere.

1. Visit Ana again.
2. Start working on Ma about not grilling Rose, or alternately, consider telling Rose about the lie—hmm, but then Rose might want to know where I had really been.
3. (More pleasant) Check on all vegetables around town. Read and memorize more from the gardening books in my possession. New idea: Ask Ana if I can see more of her garden or books at her house (Should that be #4?)

This last idea thrilled me. When I had been at Ana's house I hadn't really looked around or asked to see any of her remaining books or about what she might be growing. We had both been stunned and focused on the recent emergency surrounding Clare and Dante's disappearance. It now occurred to me that Ana must have a wealth of resources. But what about GRIM? I watched for any suspicious-looking characters whenever I went out, but honestly, it didn't seem as if I was being followed. Ana had questioned me about it, made me promise to be on guard, but had not forbidden me from visiting. In fact, we had made plans to meet again.

I thought back to the first day Clare had shown the two tiny seeds to Dante and me. *These seeds will change the world,* she had told us. I remembered thinking how overly-dramatic she seemed, yet trusting her just the same. Any doubts I ever had concerning Clare never lasted long. I thought about what had happened a few days later; how Clare had explained about GRIM and admitted to being followed and chased down an alley; her mother visited by two men in shades and suits. We had been a little scared at first, but over time, eluding the men had become a game to us. Maybe that's what growing up with the Monitor had done—desensitized us from reality. And then, when Ana saw the man outside of St. Vincent's, she had freaked—wouldn't even teach us anymore. That's when things started feeling different, like maybe this was something dangerous. Ana confessed that perhaps her association with Clare had attracted the GRIM agents to us. That's when we really understood about the secret group of which Ana was a member, the Seed Savers. If Clare had told Ana about the GRIM men visiting her mom, she probably never would have taught us.

But I was glad she had taught us. Even with Clare and Dante gone, I was glad we had learned what we had. Before Ana and her knowledge about seeds and plants, and real food, what had my life been, anyway? School, Monitor, folding paper birds, chores. Now I had purpose. Daily, I checked on the progress of *living organisms*. Plants I knew intimately—peas, carrots, lettuce—friends I'd known, grown, and nurtured from tiny seeds. I knew I'd go on to learn more, do more. Someday, I would meet other Seed Savers. Someday, we would help get the country headed back in the right direction. I was confident that Clare and Dante were okay. To be honest, I was a little jealous. What kind of adventure must they be having?

I ended my list of things to think about and do with the thing I needed to do first: I needed to tell Celia what was going on. Though I knew it was a good thing, for her sake, I wasn't sure how to break it to her. How exactly do you tell a parent that her children are involved in an illegal activity and are essentially fugitives? These lawbreakers being all of eight and thirteen years old, no less? *Buck up, Lily,* I told myself. *Clare and Dante had to be brave; you can be, too.*

And with that helpful piece of encouragement to myself, I closed my journal and got ready for bed.

"I'll take care of it tomorrow," I said to the darkness of my room.

chapter 6

THE MORNING ERUPTED bright and clear, but by mid-afternoon cool breezes had blown in clouds, darkening the day. At last a welcome relief from the heat—rare for August in these parts. I couldn't relax, knowing what lay ahead. Celia wouldn't be home until four o'clock. Over and over I practiced how the visit might go. *Oh Lily, honey, come on in. How are you? I miss my babies,* she would say. *Celia,* I would answer, *I have something to tell you.*

On and on it flowed, this conversation in my head, until I thought my brain might shatter.

I got up and wandered around the apartment. *I want to cook,* I thought. *I want to measure and chop and saute.* I'd been studying one of the cookbooks Ana gave us, looking up words I didn't know; cooking sounded like a lot of fun and a great way to take my mind off of my troubles.

Why had everything had to change? I cleaned the toilet instead.

To say things didn't go well with Clare's mom would be an understatement. Celia freaked.

"You think what??? You did what???

"Let me get this straight, behind my back, under my nose, you children planted seeds and grew vegetables? People don't do that, Lily. It's against the law." She said the last three words with extra clarity and emphasis: *Against the law.* Then a new thought registered in her eyes.

"Someone must have helped you."

I cautiously told her about the after-school sessions but refused to give Ana's name. For a moment I feared I'd made a mistake in telling her the truth, but only for a moment. Looking back, I can't blame her for the outburst; I only blame myself in not imagining her reaction more realistically.

By the time I left, some two hours later, I felt better knowing Celia understood why her children had gone away—that she was in no way to blame. I told her I had sent a message out to the secret network and to trust that a larger village of friends would be on the lookout for her kids. This meant a great deal to her. I even shared with her the children's strong faith in God. It brought tears to her eyes.

"They're good kids," she said. "They've done so much with the little I've given them."

I promised Celia I'd let her know if I found out anything new. She understood I considered myself a part of the Movement, that my mother was not to find out, and that I wouldn't tell her anymore than was absolutely necessary.

When I got out my journal that night, I made a check-mark next to "tell Celia," and looked at the other things on the list: Ana, Rose, vegetables. Not a hard choice; then again, maybe I could accomplish all three tomorrow. With the hard part out of the way, life was starting to feel better again. Well, as good as could be expected, all things considered.

I started sowing the seeds of motherly discomfort early the next morning. I figured I might as well get a head start.

"Mom," I said over breakfast squares, "I want you to meet Rose, but I really don't want you to ask her a lot of questions. Kids our age … just like to be left alone."

To my surprise, she didn't look hurt. I kept talking.

"So, anyway, is it okay if I have her come over sometime?"

"Of course, Lily. I know you are lonely without—"

She stopped abruptly. I felt my temper rising.

"*Clare*, Ma, without *Clare*. You can say her name. She'll be back, Ma. Clare and Dante will come back." I was up and moving fast to my room, slamming the door behind me.

Uncomfortable with my adolescent emotions, she did not follow me. Retrieving my journal, I began pouring out my feelings about what had just happened. I overreacted, yes, but why? I guessed it had something to do with the hormones our health teacher had told us about. I felt guilty about storming off and slamming the door, but was too humiliated and embarrassed by my actions to return. Instead, I turned to my to-do list and thought about how to combine the remaining items. If I could pull off Rose meeting my mom, could I continue to use Rose as an alibi while visiting Ana? It seemed so simple, but the deception part bothered me. But hadn't I been fooling Ma for months when Ana taught us about gardening after school? Somehow, no, that seemed legitimate. I had attended after-school tutoring at St. Vincent's. It was the subject matter she didn't know about. That wasn't really a lie, right?

It occurred to me that if Rose were to go to Ana's with me, I wouldn't be lying; I'd be totally in the clear. But this thought made me uneasy. Going to Ana's would always be for the purpose of learning gardening, and to bring in someone new was no small matter. However, it was an interesting idea, and one I jotted down to ponder later.

My angst down in blue ink across the lined paper combined with the diversion of my plotting, I felt much better. It was still early, the best time for visiting my orphanage of plants scattered throughout the city. I kissed my mom as I passed by, indicating all was forgiven. She looked penitent and I knew my outburst had actually worked in my favor. My poor mom, never knowing when I would explode. It wasn't easy for me either; it's not like we can control these things. Suddenly we aren't our sweet little girl selves anymore. Things just change.

ڶ   ڶ   ڶ   ڶ

Cool air whipped my face as I ventured up and down the streets, peering at the places concealing my renegade veggies. This weather would be a relief for my edible vegetable friends, as would the bottles of water bulging in my backpack. These plants: the guilty secret I'd kept from Clare and Dante. I couldn't help myself, and yet I felt like a liar and a cheat, never mustering the nerve to confess before their sudden disappearance. God knows I wanted to … like any deception, it started small. *I'll just plant a few of these here*, I'd say to myself. *Maybe nothing will come up. I'll tell them if and when a plant actually sprouts.* Then later on, *I'll tell them once I know it's going to survive.* And on and on. The longer I procrastinated and rationalized, the bigger the deception grew—in my case—quite literally. By early June I nibbled delicate round sweet peas and tangy red radishes. There were some days I couldn't even bear to be around Clare and Dante in my deception. I would be in denial if I said I only missed and envied my vanished friends; there was a heavy dose of guilt thrown in as well. I was the real law-breaker. I'm the one GRIM should have been watching most carefully.

I emptied the last of my water on the herbs. Despite my planting frenzy earlier in the season, I found to my disappointment that many of the seeds I'd sown yielded plants I couldn't use. Although the lettuces and chards proliferated, they didn't taste like much. From my research I realized there needed to be some preparation, but how could I do that? Even if I had what was needed at home, Ma would certainly freak if I started cooking up something or decided to eat a bowl of green leaves for lunch. And the herbs—parsley, dill, and so on—had such exotic scents, but my understanding was that they were used to flavor other food. Sometimes it seemed to me that growing and preparing your own food was indeed complicated and time-consuming and it was no wonder the old ways had died out.

As I pedaled home, I thought about Ana and all I might still be able to learn from her. My thought bubble burst, however, as I steered my bicycle into our apartment complex and there, riding around in circles, was Rose.

"Hey," she yelled, "there you are."

"How did you know where I lived?"

"You told me, Einstein, remember?"

So I had—that day at the fountain.

"Is your mom feeling better?"

I hoped she didn't see the initial look of confusion that skipped across my face before I remembered the fib I'd told about my mom. This deception business was hard to keep track of.

"Yeah, sure," I managed. "I think she was tired or overworked or something." She wasn't really listening to my answer.

"Wanna do something?" she asked.

"Okay," I said, "what?"

"I don't know."

"Monitor games?"

"I'm tired of Monitor games. I do that all the time."

"Do you have brothers and sisters, Rose?"

"A younger sister—I get tired of looking after her—that's why I sneak away when I can," she said, those green eyes sparkling and a wide smile peeling open her face.

"Wanna ride then?" A plan was hatching in my conniving head. Maybe I'd just casually ride out past Ana's with her and see if anything seemed suspicious. I really hadn't seen any GRIM agents tailing me alone, and the more I contemplated Rose, the less inclined I was to think kid spies existed. I guess there was also that

39

subconscious tempting of fate, as in, *what more could possibly happen?* After all, my two best friends had already disappeared. Maybe tempting fate was all there was left to do.

"Course," she replied, and off she darted.

She led me down the block and to the park where we'd met. We used up and spit out the decrepit bike lanes and then buzzed through the part set aside for skate boarders, much to their ire. She stayed in the lead the entire time. I had to hand it to her—the girl had stamina. At last she stopped and let me pull up alongside her.

"I'm hungry," she announced.

"Yeah, it's probably about time for lunch."

"Lunch? You mean you've already eaten today?"

"You mean you haven't?" I looked at Rose. She had an unkempt appearance I hadn't noticed before.

"We don't eat as much in the summer," she stated matter-of-factly. "The schools only serve lunch during certain weeks and no breakfasts after June. My stepmom and dad try to save money."

I wanted to say, *but what about the Food Trucks, what about government ration tickets*, but it seemed nosey. It seemed embarrassing. I said nothing.

"So," she said. "Wanna see what pack is on today over at Obama?"

Obama Elementary apparently was where the free lunches for my neighborhood were served. I had no idea about this. Me and my friends weren't rich, but on the other hand, we also never ate free community meals. This had always been a level of poverty seemingly beneath us. It was dawning on me how much we took for granted our hard-working mothers.

"Um," I faltered. "Wanna come back to my place?"

chapter 7

"ROSE, HOW NICE to meet you," my mother gushed when I introduced her. Rose shot me a glance with raised eyebrows at my mother's overdone excitement, but didn't say anything. We ate from our choice of the same three combo packs that we had every day for lunch—a balance of Vitees, Carbos, and Proteins. She even gave us Sweeties, for which I generally had to wait until mid-afternoon. Ma did well in not asking too many questions. I can't say the same for Rose, but at least she kept quiet in front of my mother.

"What's your mom's name?" she asked as we walked to our bicycles.

"Junko."

"Junko? Is that Chinese or something?"

"Japanese." I said it sort of icily, but Rose wasn't always adept at the finer points of communication.

"So you're Japanese?"

"Half Japanese. My father is regular American."

"Where's your father?"

We were next to our bikes. "Where are we going now?" I asked, trying to avoid the conversation.

"I don't know," she answered. "How 'bout you lead this time."

I hopped on and began riding. I looked around for any sign of GRIM. Rose noticed my gawking.

"Watcha looking for?"

"Spies," I said, over-dramatically.

"Oh," she said. "Right." She peered around, catching on to what she saw as a silly make-believe game. "The coast is clear," she sang out.

As we continued riding and exited the city proper, Rose called from behind.

"Lily, hold up."

I stopped.

"Where are we going?" she asked.

"Just riding," I told her.

"I never leave town."

"It's okay," I said. "I've gone this way; it's not that bad. And I don't go too far. Want to?"

"Okay," she said. "It's better with two."

After about twenty minutes, I realized that it was quite a distance to Ana's—how had I forgotten? I decided it wasn't a good idea to drag Rose out there just yet. I called back that when the traffic was right, we would do a U-turn and head back.

In town, we rode straight for the fountain to cool off.

"That was great," Rose said. "Really invigorating."

I smiled. It had felt good. Maybe this was how to do it: A few times a week, ride out of town with Rose, gradually going farther and farther, until at last we'd be at Ana's house.

Rose latched on to me like an infant around your thumb. Every day, just after lunchtime, she showed up ready to ride. She seemed to enjoy the "spy" game, always peering around and calling out "the coast is clear." Within two days we had made it to Ana's house. I had planned to buzz by and turn around, maybe do a little rubbernecking at her place; but as luck would have it, Ana was out in that blazing sun tottering around. And she waved.

I hit my brakes. Rose stopped next to me. Before Rose could open her mouth, Ana spoke.

"Lily? Is that you? And Rose?"

I wasn't sure how to proceed. Act like it was a coincidence for Rose's benefit?

"Oh, hi," Rose answered, recognizing Ana and remembering the tutoring sessions. "Ana, right? Hey, Lily, it's the lady from St. Vincent's, remember?"

Ana and I exchanged glances.

"Very nice to see you again, Lily," she said.

Ana invited us in, setting tall glasses before us.

"What kind of tea is this?" asked Rose, screwing up her face in disdain.

"I made it myself," Ana said, smiling. "You are probably used to a much sweeter tea."

"Yeah," said Rose, drinking it anyway. "How did you make it?"

Maybe I wouldn't have to make the important decisions, after all. Maybe Ana was taking the lead.

"Well, Rose, as it happens, tea is made quite easily with just water and leaves or flowers from certain plants."

Rose's eyes narrowed; her forehead wrinkled. "What?"

"You boil the water and pour it over the leaves, fresh or dried, let it set a spell, and then drink. For iced tea you'd let it cool and then put it in the refrigerator. That's about all there is to it. But most folks like it sweet. That's what you're used to. Lots of sugar."

I wondered what Rose was thinking. Ana's explanation seemed to have maintained Rose's attention as few things did. Hanging around with her in recent days I'd gotten the impression she only really listened to half of what anybody ever said. I didn't know if it was bad manners or if her brain just moved so quickly she was already heading down the next mental path, leaving behind whatever was being spoken—even if it was an answer to her own question.

"That's interesting," she said finally. "It would certainly save money if you just boil leaves in water. And if you could actually enjoy it without the sweetener. You'll have to show me how to do it sometime."

Ana smiled. "Of course. And before you ride back, you'll need some sustenance." She got up and crossed the room, pulling some Sweeties from a shelf and placing them before us.

We gratefully gobbled up the round and chewy sweets, and drank more tea. It really was pretty good, and definitely refreshing. I glanced around the kitchen, hoping to see evidence of homegrown food, but found none. Resisting disappointment's pull, I reminded myself of the glass clasped in my hands. *She's being careful*, I thought. *Just because things aren't right out in the open doesn't mean they're not here.* Ana's cat, crouched under the table, eyed me dubiously.

"Wow, that was weird, wasn't it?" Rose said as we mounted our bikes.

"What?"

"Finding her, out here. And the way she just waved, recognizing us so easily. Strange."

I tried not to look suspicious, pedaling away perhaps a bit too quickly in an effort to avoid eye contact.

It was a relief when Rose told me she wouldn't be able to come over for a few days. I desperately needed to talk with Ana alone.

chapter 8

"I SEE YOU AND ROSE seem to be getting along," Ana said soon after she welcomed me into her cozy black and white kitchen. I was falling in love with the place. It reminded me of homey scenes I'd seen on old Monitor shows. I sometimes daydreamed about standing over the stove cooking, or working at the counter preparing food—doing more than cutting the wrappers of the plastic-coated packages and heating the carefully shaped contents.

"Yeah," I acknowledged, "she's okay."

"How did things go with Clare and Dante's mother?"

I explained how my conversation with Celia had gone. Next she asked about whether I was able to send out the alert to the Seed Savers Network.

"Oh, good work, Lily. You are a true soldier in the Movement."

I blushed at the compliment. "It wasn't so hard," I muttered.

I felt a pressure, like you do on hot humid days, right before a big rainstorm, when you feel like you could cut the air into little squares with a big knife. I rose from my seat and walked toward an open back door, peering out into Ana's charming backyard.

"Ana, teach me more," I blurted. "I want to know everything. I'm not afraid. There's nothing else to lose." I felt something brush my leg. Looking down, I saw Ana's cat walking away.

Still somewhat fragile, Ana used a cane to push herself up and hobbled over to me. Standing behind me, she placed a hand on my shoulder, peering off in the same direction as I.

"Okay, Lily."

We passed through the door and into the small yard. Rather than grass, a stone path wandered through a chipped wood groundcover from which burst all kinds of green plants and flowers, many of which I recognized as herbs. We toured the yard leisurely, Ana naming each plant and telling a little about it. She showed me chamomile, from which our tea was made, underground veggies—beets, carrots, and onions—and a big leafy clump that she declared as "a most brazen act," due to its large size; but, as she explained, so forgotten by present day citizens as to be unrecognizable—some kind of squash. And finally, she pointed out the lettuce dancing among the zinnias.

"I eat a salad every day for lunch," she boasted.

She told me about how much more she used to do, and how, in recent years, she had raised plants indoors. I was excited to hear this; I really wanted to taste a ripe tomato, having lost ours just before it ripened. My excitement was short-lived, though, as Ana recounted how this year she had ceased much of her growing activities because of her interaction with us children. She wanted to protect us in every way possible.

One of the most exciting things Ana *did* show me however, was right out front. A large bush with small blue berries. As it turned out, GRIM had not cited her for this bush all those years ago. But as it also turned out, these berries were completely edible; they were called *blueberries*. There weren't a lot of bushes with berries around, except maybe holly, and everyone knew never to eat holly berries since they were poisonous (at least enough to make a person sick; I once saw a kid eat a bunch and he threw up until I thought he would turn inside out). I suppose it's one of the reasons I never thought berries were edible; they just didn't seem like food, you know? And only a short time ago the whole idea of eating *any* part of a plant seemed absurd to me. Everyone had heard of blueberry-flavored Sweeties, of course. It just didn't mean anything. You know, like other things people said: What did "hold your horses" have to do with being patient, for example? Or sounding like a "broken record" when you said something too many times ... What the heck was a broken record?

So when Ana showed me the bush and urged me to try the taut blue berries, it eased the disappointment I'd experienced about the tomatoes. The blueberries, by the way, were yummier than any Sweetie I'd ever tasted.

After a tour of both the back and front yards, we sat down where we had started—her pleasant kitchen table. Like the old books, it was a kitchen from the past—a place where food was carefully prepared, preserved, and presented.

"Ana, will you teach me about cooking and preserving?"

"Well …"

"And what about Rose?" I told her how Rose and I had been hanging out, and my mom's relief that I had a friend to do things with. I asked her what she thought about opening our secret circle to include Rose.

She had listened silently until I was completely finished—and then some. I searched her face for an answer.

At last she said, "Lily, let me think it over."

chapter 9

TRUE TO HER WORD, Rose's absence continued for the next two days. I shrewdly neglected to mention this to my mom, taking off shortly after lunch as usual, letting her think what she would. The weather was muggy and a light smog muted the summer sky, making it appear cooler than it actually was. I rode out to Ana's, expectant to learn, and glad for the time alone with her.

Ana was on her front porch rocking in a white wicker chair. A floral fragrance pleased my nostrils; downtown never smelled like this. I realized I was smiling.

"Have you eaten?" she asked as I dragged my bicycle up the steps.

"Yes," I answered.

"Oh, well I haven't. You said you'd like to learn how to prepare food; I thought maybe we could start with a salad."

My heart leaped. This was something I'd been dreaming about. All that lettuce growing around town and not knowing how to make it taste good.

"Okay," I said. "I can always eat more." I followed her in and plopped down in my now usual spot at the table. She gave me a look that made me wonder what I'd done wrong.

"Lily, *preparing* food is not the same as *prepared* food. It entails effort."

I jumped up. "Sorry."

"I have already gathered the lettuce from the garden, because it's better to do it before it gets too warm outside," she explained; "it's easier to wash when it is fresh and crisp."

Wash? Of course; you would wash food coming from a garden.

She opened her refrigerator and took out a plastic bag filled with vibrant green and red lettuce.

"This has already been washed, but let me explain the process. I like to fill the sink with water and submerge every leaf," she said, "make sure all the little critters float off."

My face betrayed my surprise. "Critters?"

She smiled. "Yes, dear. We are not the only ones who like good food. Expect an occasional worm or bug, but don't worry about it. That's why we wash it. Also, sometimes it gets dirty from watering or rain when the soil splashes up."

"But what if we miss a 'critter'?" I persisted.

"Extra protein."

I wasn't sure if this was a joke or if she was serious.

"After it's submerged, I sometimes pass each leaf under running water just to be sure, then drop it into my handy salad spinner." She took an ancient hard plastic contraption out of her dish drainer and showed me how it spun. "This helps remove some of the moisture so it isn't too soggy. Now," she said as she opened the bag, "for the salad."

Ana drew two plates from her cupboard. She tore up the leaves and placed a small pile on each plate. Opening the fridge again, she pulled out a tube-shaped green vegetable.

"Do you remember this one?" she asked as she held it up. I strained to remember. Like a foreign language, I found it hard to recall all the new words gardening introduced into my vocabulary.

"Cumber-something?"

"Cucumber," Ana said. "They're great in a salad. Radishes and tomatoes also dress it up. But I'm afraid I don't have either of those right now. However, I love the flavor fresh herbs add." She opened a drawer and pulled out a large pair of scissors. "Come along."

I followed her out the back door, nearly tripping over Mrs. Fluffbottom, the cat. Ana wove her way along the stone path, snipping here and there.

"I love a touch of dill," she said. "Basil leaves are also good. And of course, cilantro. Parsley, chives, mint; whatever you've got, and whichever you prefer." She looked so happy, so healthy, outdoor among her plants.

The herbs tucked in her apron pockets, she walked back toward the house, stopping only to cut off the tip-tops of some green onions. Once inside, she didn't even wash the herbs, but simply snipped them over our salads. Just like that—from garden to plate. The fragrance was startling.

Ana brought to the table a lovely blue glass bottle with an ornate stopper. She drizzled a shiny substance over each salad.

"A little oil to finish it."

"Oil? Like to fry stove-top packets?"

"Yes," she said. "Only I have flavored mine a bit. But with the fresh herbs we've added, you could use plain oil and still be fine."

Seated, she reached over and took one of my hands in hers. She bowed her head and closed her eyes. I did the same.

"Dear God in heaven, thank you for my special friend, Lily. Thank you for this food to nourish our bodies. Amen."

I felt her hand release mine and somehow remembered that "amen" meant "the end" in prayer language. I opened my eyes. Ana smiled at me and picked up her fork.

"Enjoy."

I watched as she slid her fork under the leaves and brought it to her mouth. I tried my hand at it. If I hadn't already munched on carrots and radishes earlier in the summer, I might not have taken to the natural and "green" taste of the salad, but since I had, I have to say I honestly enjoyed it. It reminded me of fireworks. You know, like when the big blue explosion makes you go "ahh," then suddenly off to the left and lower down there's a red burst of color, a shooting blast of purple, a loud pop, a bright light. Each new taste— cucumber, dill, onion, basil—a new and exciting unexpected shower of sparks.

"It's so good."

"Mmm," she said, "yes, it is."

After we finished our salads and set our dishes in the sink, Ana asked me to sit back down. I was anxious to know what she had decided about Rose. Every way I played it, it seemed advantageous to have Rose know about Seed Savers. And yet I also understood Ana's reluctance. It was always risky to bring in new people. Even if Rose wasn't a spy, could she keep her mouth shut? She seemed like the type who might blab the wrong thing to the wrong person.

Unfortunately, Ana seemed in no hurry to discuss the matter.

"Lily, did you bring your notebook?"

I was taken off guard. "My notebook?"

"You told me you wanted to continue learning."

"Oh. Yeah. I—um—I'm sorry. I forgot my notebook," I faltered.

"Well I suppose you are young and have a good memory," she said. "I have to write down anything new. I'd like to explain a bit about preserving food. I love fresh food," she said, "but unless you live in a place with warm and sunny weather and an adequate source of water throughout the year, you won't be able to grow your vegetables year-round—at least not outdoors. So you understand what is meant by growing seasons and when a vegetable is *in season?*"

I nodded. Yes, I thought I understood this. I had read a lot in the books we'd been given, and the experience this spring and summer with my renegade plants had given me first-hand experience about each seed's time to shine.

"Let's start with herbs, since you can see I have so many. The best way to preserve herbs—and some will grow year-round in these parts—is to dry them."

I didn't really understand what she meant.

"They're easy to dry, and retain excellent flavor. If you plan on using the leaves, you want to harvest them before the plant flowers. The best time to cut them is mid-morning. Give them a good shake to rid them of any of our friends," she said winking, "no need to wash them unless they are visibly dirty, or growing near a busy street. If you do wash them, make sure you get them as dry as possible so that they won't mold. I like to tie them in bunches and hang them upside down in a warm, dry place. This old house has a nice attic, so that's where I hang mine. It usually takes a couple of weeks, maybe longer. They should feel dry and crumbly. You can then simply run your hands up and down the stem to remove the leaves. The leaves can be stored either whole or crumbled. Whole leaves preserve the flavor better, but crumbled are easier to store. It's best to keep them out of sunlight."

From the counter she gathered some of the small glass jars and boxes which were filled with green flakes and neatly labeled.

"How do you use them?" I asked.

"Well, as you saw today, herbs and spices are used to flavor things. Your Vitees often have herbs in them for flavor. I use these when I cook up dishes. It's harder these days, without many ingredients available in Stores, but occasionally I can get something together that benefits from my herb collection. And of course dried mint and chamomile make excellent tea."

Ana let out a long sigh. "I suppose I dry way more than I can ever use; mostly it's just habit nowadays."

From my perspective, aside from the tea-making, I couldn't really think of how they might be of any use all dried up and crispy like that. Yet I wanted to try my hand at it. I just didn't know how I could pull off anything at home. Unlike Celia, who was at work so many hours every day and night, my mom was almost always home.

"Will we be drying herbs here?" I asked.

"Sure, we can do that."

The question about Rose loomed.

I looked at the clock on the wall—two hours had already passed since I had left home. I jumped up, realizing that by the time I got back I would be later than usual.

"Thanks, Ana, I need to get going."

"Lily, I won't be home tomorrow in case you were planning on coming over."

"You won't?" I don't know why I was surprised. Of course she had an active life. After all, that was how we had met, with Ana's volunteering at St. Vincent's after-school tutoring.

"I have something to do in town. Just thought I'd let you know."

"Yeah—thanks. See you later."

Ten minutes into my ride I realized the question about Rose had not been answered. And with Ana unavailable tomorrow, I might not have another opportunity to talk with her alone. Rats! How would this work out? And what would I do all day tomorrow? The last week had passed so quickly now that I was hanging out with Rose. Tomorrow I'd be on my own—no Rose and no Ana. *No Clare, no Dante,* whispered that small voice within my heart.

chapter 10

I TRIED SLEEPING IN but it didn't work. The sun appeared too early, invading my room, rousing me awake. Though out of bed, an inert depression settled over me like thick fog filling a valley. I could tell by the way Ma watched, she knew something was wrong. Thankfully, she didn't dare ask what was the matter. My adolescent crabby mood seemed to shut her down lately. Even though it was still morning and I didn't ride with Rose 'til afternoon, just knowing I had no afternoon plans dampened my spirit. At last I gravitated to my journal; I hadn't written in it for a few days. I reviewed my last couple of entries. So much had happened this summer. The disappearance of my friends, finding Ana, connecting with Rose. These were exciting and extraordinary things—how could I feel so glum?

That rational side of me once more decided to blame hormones. If this was what being a teenager was like, and my thirteenth birthday rapidly approaching, I wasn't sure I wanted to be one. Why not skip this phase altogether? If only.

I scribbled these thoughts down for today's entry, along with my misfortune about having no one to hang out with in the afternoon. And in a surprise burst, I also expressed my frustration over Ana's not answering me about Rose. However, her stalling had given me time to explore my own feelings on the issue. And I decided I wanted Ana to allow Rose into our circle. I missed Clare and Dante. I wanted to share my gardening adventures with someone again. Despite my initial doubts, I believed Rose could keep a secret. I knew what I would say to Ana if she asked my opinion. Perhaps this was why she had waited so long to answer me; maybe she was giving *me* time to process.

After I read and wrote in my journal I felt better. Reviewing and reflecting on what I'd learned from Ana inspired me to retrieve the books she'd given us, and see what I could find on herbs, squash, and preserving methods. It felt like

I was always trying to connect the dots on a page as big as the world itself.

Rereading the section on herbs in each of my books, I learned that not only could herbs be used for tea and seasoning, they could also be used medicinally, and for the pleasure of their fragrance. I wondered which kinds I had planted, and pulled out the notes I kept of my gardens. A few had not germinated: I'd had no luck with the parsley or lavender, while cilantro, basil, thyme, mint, and oregano had all come up, some more vigorously than others. A search through the books confirmed my guess that the seeds I'd sown were herbs used primarily in cooking. I checked herb preservation methods, and while Ana had taught me all about drying, she hadn't mentioned "freezing," another method listed. It was an odd thought. You could get frozen treats, and a few people owned box-sized freezers, but the idea of putting herbs or carrots, or any other kind of plant in there seemed weird. We, of course, did not own a freezer.

There had to be more. A person couldn't possibly dry every kind of vegetable, yet it was my understanding that most everything could be preserved. I looked through the books from Ana—

very little on preserving. I wondered again about the books Clare had kept at their place. I hadn't felt comfortable asking Celia, given the circumstances, but I felt certain that among the books received from Ana had been some focused on harvesting and preserving. Now that Celia knew about our activities, and time had passed since the kids' disappearance, asking about the books wouldn't be as hard. I knew where they had been kept—under Dante's bed. I set my sights on visiting Celia.

With morning over and the plan of action in my head, I no longer felt depressed about the afternoon. I cheerily made conversation over lunch with Ma to cue her that my moodiness had passed and relieve her from the dance over pins and needles. I even offered to help with the origami, explaining that Rose was busy. Of course she was happy for my help and company. We worked together silently, each thinking our own thoughts.

chapter 11

THE NEXT DAY I was fortunate to find Celia home before noon. I think maybe I woke her up, but she was happy to see me.

"Lily, come in! Sit down." Her face was hopeful. "Have you heard from my babies?"

I told her I probably would not hear from them directly, but assured her again that if I heard anything at all, I'd let her know. This was something Ana was hesitant about: my learning the process for communicating on the Network. She seemed overly cautious in this regard.

"Celia," I said, "remember how I told you about Clare and Dante and me learning to grow food?" She nodded in affirmation. "Our teacher also gave us some books ... Were any books taken when the police seized the tomato?"

Her forehead crinkled in puzzlement.

"No," she answered. "Nobody said nothin' about books. But the place was torn up real good. It's possible they took things without telling me."

"No—not if they were trying to get you in trouble. Do you mind if I look? They were in Dante's room."

"Go ahead."

We walked to the partitioned space Dante called his room. I got down on my hands and knees and peered under his bed.

Celia grinned. "I don't think even you can crawl under there."

"Let's move it," I suggested.

Back in the farthest corner we found what remained of our precious books. There were only six; those combined with my four did not equal all of our contraband books. I was certain Clare and Dante had taken some with them.

"They packed books when they ran away? I can't believe it. No, I can. Only my kids would include books in their knapsacks for running away." She shook her head, but her eyes were smiling.

"I hope you're right about all those *friends* taking care of them, Lily. 'Cuz they sure can't eat books, even if they are books about food."

I wasn't back home ten minutes when Rose showed up. I guess she thought having been absent for a few days had earned her an invite to lunch. Ma, of course, was gracious, and I figured if Rose normally ate the free school lunches, she needed every free meal she could scrounge—but I also knew it was a drain on our meager resources. I'd halfway been expecting her, though, and in truth, was happy to see her.

Over lunch, Rose complained about the days spent watching her sister and doing extra chores while her mom had been out of town. Her dad worked full-time and usually left the meals, laundry, and other tasks to her mom. Rose had to play backup whenever her mom was sick or had other things to do.

Ma complimented Rose for being such a big help to her family. I was embarrassed at her saying such a dumb thing, but Rose seemed to appreciate it. You got the feeling no one in her family had responded with ample gratitude so even the thinnest accolade from my mother was cherished. We take what we can get.

"Ready to ride?" Rose asked before I'd swallowed my last bit of teriyaki-flavored Protein.

"Sure am," I answered.

We headed in our usual direction. After about twenty minutes, Rose pulled parallel with me. "You think we'll see that old lady again—Ana?"

"Maybe."

"Should we stop, or just ride by and look?"

I'd been wondering the same thing. Ana had not answered my question. *Well, that's her problem.*

"Well?" Rose waited for my answer.

"What do you think?" I responded.

"How 'bout we ride slow and if she's out, we stop. If not, we ride by, but then stop on the way back."

"Okay," I said. "Why not? Besides, we could use the break. Even if she's not around, we could sit on the grass for a few minutes."

The yard was empty. We rode past and turned around at the next bend. On the way back, Rose pulled into the worn driveway and pedaled up to the porch, me not far behind. She dropped her bike and galloped onto the porch. She was already banging on the peeling white door before I had leaned my bike against the house. I heard Ana's voice call "coming" from inside. I reached the top of the stairs just as the door opened. Rose surprised me with that great smile of hers, the one that turned her into a pretty girl. She shone it brightly at Ana.

"We're here again!"

Ana beamed back at her. "So you are."

Once inside, Ana again offered us iced tea. This time, rather than chamomile tea, she served us mint tea—with some fresh leaves still in it. This was very exciting; for me because I was actually growing mint, and for Rose because she was so intrigued with the notion of "homemade" tea.

You can imagine my surprise, however, when Ana turned and asked if I'd remembered my notebook this time.

"I—um—" I looked at Rose, then Ana "—you know—"

Rose looked at me, "Your notebook?" She looked at Ana, "We need notebooks?"

"Lily has, in the past, taken notes on a few things I've taught her," Ana explained. "And I thought you girls were interested in learning to brew your own tea. She was here day before yesterday and I reminded her to bring her notebook."

"Lily, how come you didn't tell me?" Rose asked.

I looked at Ana for help, but her eyes only twinkled with mischief. Could this be her way of answering yes about Rose?

"I'm sorry, Rose, I guess I forgot. You know, I wasn't sure we were coming here. Right? I mean, we didn't really say we were coming here when we left the apartment."

"Yeah, that's true, I guess," she admitted. She turned back to Ana. "So you're going to teach us how to make tea right now?"

"Do you have time? I wouldn't want to keep you from home too long."

Rose and I looked at each other. I checked the time.

"Yeah, sure. We're okay." I spoke for both of us.

"Okay, follow me."

Ana plucked a straw hat from the top of her refrigerator and pulled the large scissors from the drawer. To my surprise, she marched out her front door and across the yard. There, along the edge of her lawn was a planter filled with the green pointed mint leaves. I was surprised I hadn't noticed it before. Herbs were indeed easy to overlook. *They might just be the key to our revolution,* I thought to myself.

"Here we go," she said. "Mint is a relentless plant. I try to keep it contained, lest it take over the whole yard."

"It smells good!" Rose cried in delight. "It comes like that? I thought only flowers smelled."

Ana and I laughed. It felt good to be sharing the wonder of nature with someone new. Ana cut a fistful of the leafy stems, gave them a good shake, and handed them to Rose. Back inside, Ana let the tap run over the leaves briefly. Then she filled a pot with water and brought it to a boil. She turned the burner off, dropped the mint in, put the lid on, and set a timer for twenty minutes. While we waited, she explained what would happen next.

"People who like it sweet might add sugar now. Some people say the sugar helps extract the mint flavor from the leaves. I don't care for sweetened tea, so I don't do that. After the leaves steep—that's what you call this time of waiting— we will strain them out. For iced tea, of course, you let the tea cool, and then keep it in the fridge if you have one, or serve it with ice—like you would any drink you prefer cold. It looks nice to put a fresh mint leaf in the glass when you serve it," she added, winking.

"Can you buy sugar, just plain?" Rose asked.

"Actually, you can," Ana answered. "But it's not easy to find since most food and drink products are sold totally prepared."

"I love it," Rose purred.

"Be sure and fill Rose in on the details of gardening," Ana said to me as we were getting ready to leave. "We wouldn't want her to be misinformed. People having correct information about what they are involved in is of utmost importance," she said, punching hard each word, like staccato. I didn't need to ask what she meant. I knew exactly what Ana was saying. She was leaving it up to me to share with Rose the importance of discreetness in growing and preparing food. Even talking about something as simple as making tea might lead to trouble with the government. Rose, meanwhile, gave us both a funny look at Ana's wordy salutation.

Midway back, we stopped to rest under a large oak tree.

"So you get to teach me about gardening?" Rose asked. "I really like that we can make our own tea," she continued, as I stalled, trying to figure out how I was going to say what needed to be said. "This will save us so much money. And it will help conserve the ration tickets, too, if we don't have to buy as many drinks. I wonder, do you think it's healthy?"

I couldn't help rolling my eyes. "Of course it's healthy. You saw what was in it—water and mint leaves. Rose, there's something you need to know. There's a reason people don't go around making their own Juice and Sweeties and Vitees. It's against the law." There, I said it.

"It is?"

"Yes."

"Why?"

She had me there.

"Why, Lily?"

"I don't really know," I said. I thought back to when it all began for us. Clare had been the one to bring me in. She had done the research. I wasn't really sure why it was against the law—it was just one of those things the government had decided it should be in charge of.

"I think it had to do with ownership of seeds, or safety."

"Safety?"

"Yeah, something about people dying from food not properly processed."

"Oh. I guess that makes sense. Sooo—is making tea from leaves illegal?"

When she put it that way, I wasn't even sure. I knew owning seeds and growing plants was illegal, but if you found something already growing and knew it was edible, was that illegal? To collect and use it?

"Um, I'm not sure. Listen, Rose, the important thing here is that you don't go out and tell everybody that someone is teaching you about real food and gardening. That's what could get you into trouble. And it would get me into trouble, and Ana. So, it's a secret, okay? If you want to keep learning from Ana, it has to be a secret. You don't have to decide now, you can think about it. But please don't tell anyone."

She looked at me long and hard, those green eyes drilling fire into me.

"What's there to think about?" she said, almost flippantly. "Of course I want to do it. Who cares about the stupid government?"

chapter 12

NEITHER OF US had said another word about it
for the rest of the day. But I had plenty to sort out
in my journal that night. What an exceptional
day. My visit with Celia had gone well and I now
had six more books from which to learn. And the
unexpected turn of events concerning Rose and
Ana changed everything. Suddenly I had another
co-conspirator. I found myself writing to sort out
my emotions. There was happiness and relief—I
no longer felt alone. There was also guilt and
worry—was I replacing Clare? Could Rose be
trusted? There was confusion about how much I
should share—should I tell Rose about my plants,
or check with Ana about everything? Yet I
couldn't deny the current of excitement. Though
I appreciated Clare's level-headedness and faith in

God, Rose had a tenacity and abandon that invigorated me.

"Lily?" My mother called from behind my closed door. "Lily—what you doing in there?"

"Just thinking, Ma."

"Why not think out here?"

There she was, suspicious again about me writing. I already wasn't allowed a Monitor in my room. Obviously I couldn't read gardening books in front of her, and for whatever reason she disliked my journaling. This made writing very difficult during the summer when I couldn't use studying as an excuse.

"Okay, Ma. I just wanted to write a bit."

I heard her clicking her tongue in disapproval as she walked away.

I wasn't expecting Rose when she showed up on Sunday, though I should have guessed she wasn't a regular church attender like Clare and Dante. As we left my place, I explained to her that Ana would probably not be home since she came into town on Sundays for church. Rose was quite interested to learn this. One thing led to another and before long I had spilled the whole story of how Clare met Ana in church, our after-school tutoring/gardening classes, Seed Savers, GRIM, all of it.

"Is that what happened to Clare and Dante," she gasped, "GRIM got them?"

"No, no," I said. "I'm sure they took off because of GRIM, but GRIM didn't *get them*. It wouldn't make sense. Because I'm still here, Ana's still here. I think Clare panicked when they arrested her mom. Somehow she thought it would help her mom for them to leave."

"So have you heard from them?"

"No," I admitted. "Not yet. Ana hasn't told me how to totally connect with the Seed Savers Network. Rose—this is really serious stuff. It feels like I already told you too much."

We were in the park, watching kids splash in the fountain. Rose looked around. I saw it then. A new suspicion replacing the innocence. I knew who she was looking for. A pinprick of pain pierced my heart knowing what I'd taken from her.

"Come on, Rose, I have something to show you." As long as she knew the whole story, I saw no reason to keep my outlaw plants a secret. I jumped up and ran along the path. Next to some bushes, in a place that wasn't well-tended by the mostly volunteer staff, I pointed out what might pass for weeds: cilantro, basil, and thyme.

"For tea?" she asked.

"No, I don't think for tea. But good for adding flavor to other food dishes."

She broke off some leaves and tasted them.

"Interesting," was her only comment.

We went to another place in the park.

"Mint!" she cried. I was impressed she had remembered. "We can make our own tea, Lily!"

"Shh!" She had spoken too loudly in her excitement.

We walked back to our bikes, talking in hushed tones. I pointed out the problem with making our own tea—both of us lived in apartments where other people were always home.

"What about Clare's place? Didn't you say you told her mom everything and that she was good with it?"

"You mean ask Celia if we can carry on illegal activities at her home, having recently been busted and jailed?"

"Yeah, okay, so maybe not."

Still, I sometimes thought the visits to Ana's weren't much better. If GRIM was still watching her or watching me … But I couldn't think of any better options. Broaching the subject of gardening with Ma seemed impossible. It would be right up there with, "Say Ma, I'm thinking of writing for the school newspaper." There were some things in life not worth doing just to avoid the conversations needed to get there.

We rode to all of the vacant lots, waysides, and stacked tires where I had planted seeds. I showed her areas that hadn't worked and plants that flourished. We ended up back at my place behind closed doors where I shared my notes, sketches, and books. It was a lot for one day. After she left, butterflies did the tango in my stomach. I hoped I hadn't made a mistake.

chapter 13

"HOW ARE YOU GIRLS, TODAY?" Ana asked as we sat down for tea.

"Good," I said.

"She told me everything," Rose stated bluntly, referring to me. "Don't worry, I can keep quiet."

Ana's eyes took in all of Rose. You wonder sometimes, about old people, the way they look at you, size you up, but don't say what they're thinking. Some kind of wiseometer.

"Yes, Rose," she said at last, "I believe you can."

I had no way of knowing that what Ana saw in Rose was herself so many years before.

"Ana, we brought notebooks today," I said.

"Good, let's get started. Lily, you remember I taught you a little about drying as preservation?"

I nodded.

"Though drying, or dehydrating, is good for herbs and fruit, it's not as good for vegetables. It can be done, but I never cared much for the taste. Freezing was my mother's preferred method because the vegetables tasted more like fresh produce. It's not a viable option for us these days, however, because of storage. The government would be suspicious if an old woman like me had a large freezer, using too much power. So most of my preservation is canning. It takes a few pieces of special equipment and the knowledge of how to do it, but otherwise, it's fairly straightforward, and the vegetables last a long, long time."

Ana stood and walked to the counter. She reached into a canvas bag and pulled out two glass jars. One was filled with green beans, and another with round, bright red orbs.

"Are those tomatoes?"

"Yes," she said. "Canned tomatoes and canned green beans. Listen while I try to explain the basics."

On account of Rose, Ana went back and summarized that if a person grew more food than could be eaten fresh, there were various ways to preserve the extra to use later. She briefly covered drying and freezing, and then went into depth about canning. She reminisced about her mother preserving the harvest each summer and fall; how they rarely bought fruits and vegetables from the stores (although those stores were not the same as our Stores today). Though she had helped her mother with the canning, she had never done it herself and had only learned later on when it was almost an illegal act to do so. Then Ana carefully described the jars, special lids, large pots and "boiling water baths." It sounded difficult, and I wondered if I could ever do it. Could I be so brave to learn how, and then follow through without messing up? If I didn't do things right the food could end up toxic.

Ana read my apprehension.

"Don't be afraid, Lily, it isn't so hard. It's just a new thing to learn, like all new things."

Rose asked a lot of questions and scribbled profusely in her notebook.

After Ana had finished, I managed to bring up the subject of contacting Clare and Dante. I told her I had visited Clare's mom again to get more books. I mentioned that Celia would feel better if she heard the kids were okay. Ana nodded in understanding.

"They're okay," she said. "You may tell her they are safe."

"You've talked to them?

"Not directly, no. But when I was in town on Friday I connected with the Network. The children have traveled north. They have found friends."

It was obvious she did not want to elaborate. Her coldness on the subject not only kept me from asking more, but even subdued the normally rapacious Rose.

"Oh good," I muttered. "I'll let Celia know."

By then it was time to hit the trail. Rose and I thanked Ana for her lessons and lit out toward home.

Not in a hurry to return to her apartment, Rose hung out with me. Ma was reading her Japanese magazine on her mini-Monitor as she did every afternoon. We settled into my room.

"Let's see those books again," Rose directed.

I got out the books from Ana, including those I'd recently rescued from beneath Dante's bed.

"I need to learn everything," she said. "Show me everything Ana taught you."

We pawed through them: gardening books, cookbooks, seed saving manuals, the book dedicated solely to preserving—the one I'd been searching for but hadn't yet had time to peruse.

"So this is how people learned how to do stuff before the Monitor?"

"Yeah, I guess."

"I like it," she said. "We don't have many books at our house. And the cheap Monitors are always having problems. Too bad they don't teach how to do stuff in school."

"Yeah, school is more about knowledge than life skills. And growing your own food is blocked on the Monitor, anyway," I said.

"I still don't get that. What else don't we know about?"

I laughed. "You got that right. I mean, it's like nowadays we don't even know what it is we don't know!"

chapter 14

Our schedule varied only slightly in the following days. Rose and I started spending morning hours together tending the edibles I'd grown throughout town. I suppose it was our camaraderie that caused us to be sloppy, and our enthusiasm that got us noticed. Not to mention the too-obvious routine of it all. We were as regular as the tide. One day, just after we left the park and on our way to one of my vacant lot tire plantings, Rose took a wrong turn. When I called to her, she yelled back, "Follow me!" and rode off of our normal path, dodging into an alley.

"What's going on?" I asked when I caught up —part worried, part annoyed.

"We're being watched."

I felt my eyes widen, my mouth drop open. "What? When? Who?"

She shrugged her boney shoulders. "A kid."

"A kid? Rose! You scared me. I thought you meant GRIM, or the police."

"Who says he's not?"

"Well ... I don't know ... "

"Same kid, last three days. At first he just watched us when we took care of our plants in the park. Today he started to follow us out of the park. But I lost him pretty easily back there," she said, tilting her head.

I blushed. I hadn't noticed anything. Here I was, the old pro, and it was Rose who was keeping an eye out for enemies.

"So what now?" I asked.

"I don't know, I came here so we can talk about it."

We had dismounted and were walking our bikes slowly down the lane. A man exited the back door of his house and started banging on an old car in the alley. We got back on our bikes and rode until we found a better location to talk—the rear steps of a crumbling elementary school, not far from where we had started.

"Well?" she asked.

"I don't know," I repeated. "What did he look like?"

"Like this."

We both jumped at the rather deep and slightly accented voice. A boy of about fourteen or fifteen stepped around the edge of the building. He was tall enough, with dark wavy hair and straight white teeth. Briefly he extended his right hand, as if offering to shake, then, on second thought, pulled it back and stuck both hands into the front pockets of his jeans.

"My name is Arturo. You no need to run from me."

Rose was already on her feet. She stepped toward him rather than away.

"Oh, yeah, Arturo?" She said his name wrong —Artero—not like he'd said it, Artoorro, with a firm *u* sound and that special little trill on the *r*. "Why were you watching us? Seems pretty creepster to me."

He looked around, checking to see if we were alone.

"I know what you are doing," he whispered. "I grow vegetables, too."

Rose backed down; neither of us had expected this. We were struck silent—the moment someone hands you a gift when you were expecting a scolding.

"You do?" I finally managed to say.

"Yes," he said. It sounded like *jess*.

"Where?" demanded Rose.

"My house," he said. "Will you like to see?"

Honestly, I wanted to go. There was something about Arturo that made me trust him. But, intuition aside, Lily Gardener is nothing if not rational and methodical. You simply do not go home with strangers.

"Oh, um, not now," I stammered. "We have things to do."

"Yeah," spit Rose, "what she said."

For the life of me, I couldn't figure out why Rose was being so impolite.

I was on my bike already, pushing off, Rose right behind me. "Bye," I said. "Nice to meet you," I added instinctively.

He smiled. "With pleasure."

We ate at the apartment and though I wanted to talk to Rose about Arturo, I didn't dare mention it around Ma. Finally we finished and retreated to my room.

"What did you think of him?" I asked.

"Who?"

"You know, *the guy*."

"Artero? I guess maybe he's not a GRIM stooge—but he could be ya know. But I don't think so. I'm not even sure he's 'legal' if you know what I mean."

Of course I knew what she meant. Lots of immigrants sneaked into our country every day. It may not be the paradise it once was, but with global climate change displacing so many, and our secure government, and the sheer size of the nation, it was still a desirable place. It was a rude thing for Rose to say. I was seeing a side of her I hadn't yet encountered.

"He seemed nice," I said. "And I can't believe he grows vegetables. Rose, what if there are more people around who know about real food than we figured? Maybe things really can change. You know, this is what Ana was preparing Clare and Dante and me for—for a time when everybody was free to grow their own food *if they wanted to.* I think we should get to know him."

"Yeah, well, he'll probably still be creeping on us tomorrow," she said disgustedly. "Come on, let's head to Ana's. She said we could cook today."

As promised, Ana let Rose and I prepare some food. We picked the squash—zucchini it was called—and sliced it into thin rounds. She introduced us to another underground treasure: garlic, which we cut up tiny and quickly stirred in hot oil. After that, we added the zucchini and some salt. We cooked it on high heat—not long— just until it was browned and not too soft. We loved the fragrance of the garlic as we minced it and then again as it cooked. At last we sat to try our very first cooked meal of something not wrapped in plastic, sealed in a box, and bought at a Store. I had forgotten to warn Rose about Ana's custom of praying at meals but I need not have worried, Rose caught on right away. I wondered how she knew.

Rose and I watched Ana for a cue as to how to eat the zucchini.

Ana inhaled deeply. "Smells divine," she said. "I never grow tired of the aroma." She placed a fork-full in her mouth and chewed. "Mmm. Fine job, girls, fine job."

Rose tried hers. She nodded her head. "Good," she declared. "Yeah. I really like the brown edges."

It was different. Definitely it was better than the processed Vitees I normally ate. But it wasn't like what I'd eaten so far—the carrots, salad, radishes. It was too soft for me. Maybe I was just used to my vegetables uncooked.

"Well, Lily?" They were both watching me, waiting for my opinion.

"Um ... it's good," I said.

They didn't push. We all finished our plates and lingered over the mint tea.

"Thank you so much for teaching us," I said. "This is a dream come true. I just wish—no offense—" I said turning to Rose "—I just wish Clare and Dante were here."

"Of course," Ana said.

"Ana, why won't you teach me how to communicate with the Seed Savers Network? Not just sending an alert, like before, but to *really communicate.*"

A cloud passed over Ana's face. This had been a subject she'd been avoiding ever since I'd first asked. Initially, I had thought it was because the process was so complicated, but the more she had avoided this conversation, the more I believed she was hiding something, and I didn't understand what, or why.

"Lily—" she glanced up at the clock "—isn't it time you girls head back?"

I sighed. I was frustrated, but she was right. The cooking lessons had consumed our time as we had consumed the zucchini.

"Yes," I said. "We need to go. But Ana, I think it's time you told us everything. You said once that you never know how much longer we have together; please tell us next time?" It was a low blow—Clare would never have done it—but I felt I had to push. After all, I had not yet learned how to actually save seeds. Maybe there was a special process involved in the saving of seeds. I *did* need to be able to communicate with the others in case anything happened.

"Okay, Lily," she answered, looking and sounding old. "I'll think about it."

chapter 15

THE NEXT MORNING Rose didn't show up to ride around and help with the plants. I thought about staying home. One day wouldn't hurt; if anything needed watered or harvested, it would endure one more day. But I had anticipated seeing Arturo again, and *that* couldn't wait one more day.

My first stop was a vacant lot near our apartment complex. I had a lot of things planted there, including green beans. To tell the truth, the beans were so odd-looking I wasn't always comfortable getting close. However, the fruit on the plants—long stringy pods—was growing large and I was sure it needed picking soon. Each time I checked, the bean-fruit seemed to have increased in size. Still, I felt awkward. What if GRIM was watching? The fact that Rose had noticed Arturo following us while I had remained completely oblivious unnerved me. The beans would have to wait until I had a plan.

I peeked at the various herbs, chards, and lettuce fighting it out with the weeds in the lot, and sprinkled the slightly wilted plants with the water I'd brought. The lettuce had grown tall and was forming little blossoms; the leaves seemed smaller and I thought how much it looked like the weeds surrounding it. Glancing around carefully, I saw no sign of either GRIM agents or Arturo. In fact, there was virtually no one about and very little traffic, either. From there I rode to the main park—the one with the fountain, and always alive with kids, dogs, and the occasional vagrant. I had several good crops growing here. As counter-intuitive as it seemed, I felt less conspicuous with my plants here than elsewhere. It didn't look odd to be seen wandering around, poking about in a park; doing that in a vacant lot was inherently suspicious.

There was nothing sneaky about him; Arturo was seated on a bench in front of where pigeons gather, an old man snoozing away on his shoulder. I walked by, trying not to laugh.

"Hi!" he called out, startling the man awake.

I looked back, surprised he had called. He jumped up and moved extremely close to me in a flash.

"Where's your friend?"

"Uh—she didn't show up today. Sometimes she babysits her sister."

He must have sensed my nervousness, as he stepped farther away.

"What's your name?" He asked.

"Lily."

"Lily," he repeated, "I like that. My name is Arturo … in case you forgot."

We kept walking, but the conversation died. It was awkward. For all her nastiness, I wished Rose were there. Or better yet, Clare; Clare would have known what to say. Clare had friends who were boys. Me, I didn't know how to be around them. Dante was okay, but he was Clare's little brother— it didn't really count.

"So," he finally said. He didn't say anything more. I listened; I listened really hard. I so wanted him to keep talking. Anything.

I opened my mouth. "So?" I asked.

He whispered, "Do you visit your *jardin* every day?"

I loved the way he talked. Just a light accent, a grammar error here and there ... a Spanish pronunciation like *jardin* instead of garden.

"Yeah," I said, "pretty much."

"Me, too," he said. "I mean with *mi jardin*, not *yours*," he clarified. "Although less, now, in late summer. In the spring, when it's just beginning—every day. Every day. Even before anything—how you say—before I see anything."

I thought back to when we first planted the carrot seeds outside of Clare's apartment, how we walked by twice a day, just to see if anything was sprouting. I nodded. "Yeah, I know what you mean."

"Do you mind," he asked, "if I walk with you now as you view your plants?"

My apprehensiveness kicked in; I stopped. "Arturo, you know that it is ... " I searched his face openly for the first time, grasping for the right words, wondering if he knew the trouble I could get into.

"Illegal?" he said.

When he said it, the word meant something more. The tinge in his voice made me realize that it was a word which had been used on him, or at least on his people. I looked away, ashamed and embarrassed.

"Yes."

"I am aware," he said.

I was still trying to figure out whether or not he was angry when his voice changed back, softened, lost the edge. "So I can accompany you or not? I promise we will be careful. I know all about the laws, Lily. Believe me."

There wasn't time for me to think. To write. Only the moment.

"Sure," I said.

I don't know how long Arturo had been watching Rose and me, but he knew where everything was. I mean *everything*. And he knew *what* everything was. Later that day, as I reflected on the morning, I was again amazed at how transparent my gardening had been to anyone who was paying attention. It was eerie. And in light of what I would later learn, downright frightening.

After lunch I headed for Ana's. If Ana had any qualms about teaching me to access the Seed Savers Network in the presence of Rose, today would be an ideal opportunity. I felt I'd made my point the last time, and that Ana would finally relent and give me this last thread of information. After all, hadn't she already given us a paper with names and addresses?

Ana was surprised to see me alone.

"Rose?" she asked simply.

"Don't know. Sometimes she just doesn't show up. Her family."

"Do you not communicate with her?"

"Like texting?" I asked.

"Whatever it is you kids do these days," Ana said.

"No. Most of that stuff is too expensive or doesn't work so good. And I don't like carrying a telecom. We usually just find each other."

"Lily, why is it you are so intent on learning how to connect with the Network?"

"So I can communicate with Clare! And you know, the others—just in case." I felt too ashamed to finish my sentence. Like it might be bad luck to mention the possibility of anything happening.

"Clare and Dante are not communicating directly on the Network, Lily, it's too risky."

I couldn't think of anything to say.

"There's a reason I haven't told you everything. I shouldn't even be allowing you to visit my home."

What? Her words seemed unduly harsh.

"Where does your mother think you are now?"

Why is she asking me this? "With Rose, riding bikes."

"Have you ever spoken to your mother about gardening?"

I thought about earlier in the year, when I learned what my last name, Gardener, meant. How I couldn't help myself. I'd gone home and told Ma all about it. She had listened in a cold silence and after I'd finished talking said only, "That is true. But there are no such things as gardeners anymore. Our food comes from Stores. Farmers work for the government. Forget Gardener. It is only a name, like Goldsmith. We have jewelers now, not goldsmiths. Only a name." I had been hurt, and like so many things before, had never broached the subject again. The topics I was not allowed to speak of with my mother were vast, like so many castoff objects shut up in an attic or buried deep in a basement.

"No," I said, "not really. My mom is very law-abiding." I couldn't hide the bitterness seeping into my voice.

"Lily, dear, I'm so sorry. I haven't been open with you."

I didn't like the intensity of Ana's eyes. Suddenly, I was afraid.

"When Clare brought you to tutoring that first day, I could tell just by looking at you that you were James's little girl. I didn't need to hear your last name. But what could I do? Tell Clare you were not welcome?"

Did she just say "James's little girl?" Ana knew my father?

"What?"

"I said, what could I do? I couldn't tell Clare that she wasn't welcome to bring her best friend." She smiled.

"Why wasn't I welcome? You knew my father?"

"Oh, Lily. Lily, what does your mother tell you about your father?"

"Not much. Wait, *you knew* my father—how did you know my father?"

"James Gardener was a leader in the Seed Savers Movement."

I gasped. *What? My father? How could this be?* She continued as I listened silently, too shocked to speak.

"About fifteen years ago, before you were born, your dad was instrumental in unifying the groups around the country who wanted to change the government policy on seed ownership, gardening, food laws, etc.

"Back before that, when new food regulations had begun to gain a foothold and most people were pacified into buying and eating overly-engineered and processed food, there had been a contingent who persisted in wanting "organic" food; and plenty of farm families still knew how to grow and preserve food. It was these folks who fought the ordinances, staged the protests. But the small sit-ins and food freedom protests were merely a bother, an irritant, nothing the government really had to worry about. After a while the movements died as people tired of protesting and lost hope of making a difference. Your father, however, was just coming of age when the protests garnered massive news coverage. It was before the Monitor was reigned in—back in the "wild west" days of social media, when anyone and everyone could communicate instantly around the world. Do you even know about that Lily? Have you any idea how easy it once was?"

She paused, looking deeply into me. I shrugged. I didn't really understand. I knew the Monitor was pervasive in everyday life, but not in this interactive, real time sense she seemed to suggest. A lot of special licensing was required to engage heavily in two-way Monitor transactions. I had supposed this was one reason Ana was hesitant about teaching me—because it would undoubtedly involve more unlawful activity.

"Anyway, as I was saying, your dad was about your age when the final nail in the coffin of food freedom was pounded in. Seed ownership was officially banned, along with growing food without government authorization. Although James's family had never gardened, his grandparents had, and he had enjoyed eating rare homegrown, home cooked meals every holiday and whenever else he stayed with his grandparents. He had watched intently the coverage of the protests popping up all over the country, and wished he were among those camped out in front of the Stores or in parks. A lasting imprint was made on young James. Ten, fifteen years later, he found himself at the forefront of a movement that had gained strength underground. And it was his skill as a writer that united the thousands of disparate protestors together in the group now referred to as Seed Savers."

I was completely stunned. My own father had been a leader in Seed Savers. Suddenly my mind shot to my mother. My quiet, hardworking, innocent mom. Where was she in all of this? Before I could speak, Ana continued her explanation.

"After the social media sites were regulated and communication regressed to much the way it had been a hundred years earlier, your father began writing an underground newspaper for Seed Savers. It was distributed the old-fashioned way—by hand—and since GRIM hadn't thought anyone would go to the trouble, it spread swiftly across the country under their radar. A new, stronger movement was coming onto the scene."

As she spoke on, terror and fear gripped me. I could feel the cold white fingers wrapping around my heart. How had my father died? What had happened?

"Stop!"

Ana was startled. So was I. I hadn't realized I had spoken. My hands covered my ears. Ana was silent.

"Yes?" she finally said.

"It's too much," I managed. "Too much all at once. I … I … need to leave."

Without saying goodbye, I had gotten up and walked out. I walked my bike a good half mile before I climbed on. I walked because I was crying too hard to see well. This story Ana had told me … how could I make sense of it? When I eventually arrived home, I had gained the necessary time and distance to be able to stride into the apartment and greet my mother with a straight face. I took a long drink of water and headed to my room. This would require a lot of writing.

chapter 16

I DIDN'T LEAVE THE APARTMENT on Wednesday. I was grateful Rose didn't show up, but also slightly worried. Had something bad and unexpected happened to her family? My humming adolescent brain, however, had too many other thoughts vying for attention to give more than a passing thought to my missing friend.

What was I going to do? Should I confront my mom? No. No, I needed to hear the rest of the story. And as difficult as it was, I'd rather hear it from Ana. I stayed in my room most of the day, telling Ma I didn't feel well. The weather was humid hot—stifling, which meant wind and rain soon. What would happen to our bike rides to Ana's once the weather changed? Then again, hadn't the weather already changed? My life this year was a series of storms broken only by intermittent periods of sunshine.

I spent the day thinking, writing, reflecting. I even tried meditation of the Buddhist tradition, and a stab at Clare and Ana's style of prayer—anything to clear my mind and feel calm.

I got out the few treasured photos I owned of my dad and mom together. I wanted to remember him.

"What did you do?" I asked him. "Was it worth it?"

On Thursday, Rose again failed to show up. It was unnerving, but at least I could find out what happened to my dad in private. Clare I would have wanted by my side; Rose, Rose was still too new.

The thunderstorm had rolled in late, leaving everything wet, but at least the rain was finished. I decided to head to Ana's early. I figured chances were good she would be home, and I knew with the rain, my plants had been watered.

My risk paid off. Ana was home and didn't seem surprised at my early arrival.

"Good morning, Lily. I missed you yesterday. Have you heard from Rose?"

"No," I answered. "She didn't come over yesterday. I didn't feel good, anyway. I'm a little worried about her. Maybe her mom's sick or something."

"Yes," she agreed, nodding. "'Tis concerning."

"Ana, I'm sorry about last time. I was so overwhelmed by what you were telling me. You gotta understand, my mom never told me anything about my dad. I don't even know how he—" I swallowed; it was so hard to say "—how he died."

She was listening and nodding understandingly. Suddenly she stopped, the lines on her face rearranging themselves.

"You dear child, your father isn't dead."

chapter 17

THE LIGHT THROUGH THE WINDOWS swirled briefly and dimmed. I heard a gasp, a scream. Nothing.

I woke up with a warm hand holding mine. She must have felt a slight movement.

"Lily?"

I opened my eyes. I was still on Ana's couch—slouched in a seated position.

"What happened?"

"You blacked out," Ana said.

"How long?"

"Just a few moments. Here, drink this." She pushed some cold tea toward me. "I'm worried about you, dear. I won't let you ride back unless I know you're okay. I can drive you. Or maybe … " She stopped.

"Maybe?"

"Maybe I should call your mom."

My mom. It came back to me now, why I was here, slumped on this couch, the look of concern on Ana's face. The reason I blacked out. I pulled myself up and sipped the soothing liquid.

"I'm okay. Really."

"You thought your father was dead?" she asked.

I nodded, nursing the glass in my hands—something to clasp onto as the rest of my life fell away. When I found my voice, it was a whisper.

"All Ma ever said was, 'He is no longer with us. Do not speak it again.' I thought she meant he had died. I thought it hurt her too much to talk about it." I laughed a small, bitter laugh. "Guess I was wrong."

Yeah, I guess I was wrong; wrong about my father, wrong about my mother. My mom had let me believe for my whole life that my dad was dead. The sense of betrayal I felt was palpable. I wondered how I would ever trust her again. Anger and grief wrestled within me; an indescribable feeling of loss at the years I'd missed knowing him. Yet, then again, the wonder of the resurrection of the dead, knowing a different future had opened up in front of me. I had a father. I would know him. And maybe I would forgive Ma someday. But not yet.

"Lily, I'm sorry that you never knew your father. And I guess—under the circumstances—I understand why your mother led you to believe your father had passed away. Your mother lost a lot and she couldn't bear losing any more. The way she has lived over the years has been to protect you. It's all been for you. Please remember that."

"Ana, if you don't mind, maybe you can just pick up the story where you left off. Tell me where my father is, what happened."

"Yes, of course. How far had I gotten?"

"You told me how, after the government took over all food production, my father was able to unify protestors by writing some underground newspaper."

"Yes. That's right, the *Keeper*. It was all working so well. People across the nation were saving and exchanging seeds. More and more folks were starting to plant edible landscaping—including me. Your father wrote columns encouraging those of us who still had the skills and knowledge of planting, harvesting, preserving, and saving seeds to teach the younger generations. He wrote "how to" columns. He was instrumental in establishing and connecting groups across the country; we called them "pods," our little seedpods. Most of us felt we would have enough supporters in a few years to make political change and win back our freedoms."

"What happened?" Now that I knew my father was alive, I wasn't afraid to ask.

"What happened was Trinia Nelson. James, your father, was working hard—too hard I always thought. Someone in our group met this young woman, Trinia—short blonde perky type—and thought she was a candidate for the Movement, maybe even for a leadership role. She wasn't from around here. James was hesitant to bring her into the circle. She stayed around, kept complaining about the government polices, showed an interest in the old ways of food production. Eventually James told her about Seed Savers and invited her into the group; she had gained his trust. She caught on to gardening very quickly and was extremely dedicated and eager. Her enthusiasm didn't end with the Movement, though. She was equally attentive to your father in a more personal way."

"Like, they were dating?" I asked.

"Your father and your mother were already an item."

"My mom?"

"You seem surprised. Your mom didn't get any recognition as being a leader in the Movement, but in truth, she was one of our best teachers. In Japan, people were still allowed to grow food, and your mom was from the countryside. She still knew the old skills. Your mom taught your dad and others many things."

"Ana?"

"Yes?"

"This story you're telling me—were you there? Were you a part of this group?"

"Yes."

"So you actually *knew* knew my dad? And you know my mom?"

She nodded. "I do."

Well, now there was definitely something to think about. Ana and my mom already knew each other. My mom already a Seed Saver and a gardener. I shook my head. Nothing made sense.

"Shall I continue?" she asked.

"Uh, yeah, of course." She might as well. It couldn't get any stranger.

"As I was saying, Trinia Nelson was determined to win your father away from your mother."

I felt myself disliking this phantom from the past.

"But try as she might, she was unsuccessful. When her attempts at seducing him failed, she tried harder to climb the leadership ladder. It was obvious she was attempting to place herself in a position of power. Most of us thought she was just ambitious. Looking back, it's clear she was trying to collect enough information to deal a death blow to the Movement, squashing us forever."

"She was a spy?"

Ana nodded. "An interesting thing about Ms. Nelson to us, it seemed back then, was that she was an absolute technology whiz. And though illegal, difficult, and highly dangerous, she wanted your father to take his underground newspaper and all of the Network online. She convinced him she could crack into the system and not get caught. She told him it would be just like in the old days—people everywhere would be able to connect via the Monitor and a worldwide revolution would happen. She flattered him about the power of his writing and told him to trust her."

"And Dad believed her?"

"He took it to a small group of us. He didn't want to be responsible for the decision. By this time James and Junko were married. Trinia was at the meeting to present her plan. Her blue eyes sparkled. She tossed her bobbed blonde hair around. She quoted 'research' and praised James's writing skills, pulling all kinds of quotations out of her hat: *words are potent weapons, words are the most powerful thing in the universe, words are the tools, the nails,* etc. She used her technological prowess to impress and wow us with her presentation.

"Only one person remained unconvinced: your mother. It wasn't in your mother's personality to be direct or confrontational, however. Mostly she questioned two things that night in front of everyone: (1) the danger in putting so much information online, and (2) the need. Your mom pointed out that the Movement was already doing well. I remember the humble yet strong way your mother voiced her concerns. She was so serious. She came across as cold, negative. But that's not what it was. It was the knowledge, the deep knowing, that we would soon be going down a very difficult road if we listened to this Delilah. All the hard work our group had done—minimized and ridiculed by this woman—would be wasted, flushed down the toilet. Lives would be sacrificed and ruined, and the Movement would be set back. Your mom discerned this, yet also understood Trinia's persuasive power, and it made her tired. The normally beautiful and serene Junko was not seen that night. In her place was a woman barely recognizable, burdened as she was with the future she glimpsed on the horizon. I'm not sure if she suspected Trinia was an agent, or if she simply knew how dangerous the plan was. Trinia, of course, tossed back her head and laughed after your mom finished speaking.

"'Oh, Junko,' I can hear those words even now, 'your hormones are out of whack with the pregnancy; don't be such a negative Nancy. You should be James's biggest cheerleader.' She actually used those words, *biggest cheerleader*; even then I felt like gagging the way she demeaned your mother. She walked over and put her hands on James's shoulders as she said it. It was just awful. Your mom got up and walked out."

Ana stopped, as if that were the end of the story.

"My mom was pregnant with me?"

"Yes, sweetheart."

"So, so what happened?"

"Well, after your mother left, Trinia urged us to vote. Her powerful presentation and trivialization of your mother's concerns worked; a majority voted to go online. It was a setup from the beginning. Trinia made sure names and other identifiers of Seed Savers were part of the upload. What she said would happen, happened. For about nine hours the Network was open and ubiquitous. Seed Savers around the world were urged to "sign in"—long enough for those in countries such as ours to be rounded up and jailed or fined, all of their books, seeds, and plants destroyed. By the time we realized what was happening it was too late—the damage was done. Trinia was long gone before we understood we'd been set up; that it was all a trap. Your dad had the most charges against him; he was considered a leader at the national level and an insurgent against the government. He was sentenced to forty-five years in prison. They wanted to send your mother to jail too, but she pleaded with them on account of her pregnancy. She promised the judge that she would never break the law again. Your dad was incarcerated five days after you were born."

Too much. Too much. My dad. My mom. Ana. The Movement. Trinia Nelson. Clare and Dante. Rose. Arturo. The past. The present. The future.

"Lily—are you okay?"

"I—I—it's so much, Ana. How can I face my mom? Were you close? Why didn't you mention any of this before? Where is my dad?" The questions flowed from me like a burst dam.

"None of us knows for sure, but we think your father is being kept at a facility in Cuba. He has always been considered high risk."

"Does my mom know?"

"I don't know. As far as I know, they have never communicated. Your mom has fulfilled her agreement. She has been a model citizen. In fact, after the crackdown, GRIM agents only stayed around here for about sixteen months. We were hit so hard and so decisively in this region, broken and demoralized, that it has taken longer for us to rebound than other places. We weren't even enough of a threat to be watched. At least that's what I thought until this spring. Now you understand why I stopped meeting with you children once I encountered the GRIM agent outside the church."

"And now?"

"I've been pondering that, Lily. Why, for example, the agents seem to have left. Why they were more concerned with Clare than with you? Surely they realize you are James's daughter. Has anyone you don't know visited your apartment?"

"Not that I know of…"

Ana shook her head slowly. "Perhaps they are convinced your mother would never risk losing you by becoming a Seed Saver again. But they suspected you children were gardening and rightly guessed an adult had to be working with you. Celia would be an obvious suspect." She locked her eyes on me. "Then again, maybe they haven't left town."

I felt the joy of the past couple of weeks slipping away like old wash water down a sink. A new and stronger distrust that made the earlier GRIM-ditching days with Clare and Dante feel like child's play was clouding over my summer.

"Lily, I don't think you should ride out here anymore; I'm sorry. I've been wanting to tell you, but couldn't think of how."

I thought of my plants all over town. Then Rose. Arturo. The flagrant and thoughtless way I had been carrying on. I didn't know. I didn't know.

"I understand," was all I said.

chapter 18

IRONICALLY, the spot I found the most solace—with my plants—was now questionable in terms of safety. A part of me, the really wild "in your face" part, urged me out. *This will not be taken from you,* it said.

As I rode through town, the wheels in my head spun in sync with the wheels of my bike. Three days ago I was feeling pretty good about my life. I had a new friend, I was learning to cook, I had beans ready to harvest. Now, I didn't feel safe leaving the apartment. I was second-guessing everything: What had I gotten Rose into? My mom? Maybe I was even putting my father in danger.

My father, James Gardener. He's alive! He's been alive all of this time. And he's a *Seed Saver*.

And a writer. I smiled in spite of myself. I was like my father.

I began at the far end of the park and walked slowly down the sidewalk, peering cautiously around. I took breaks on the benches and then sat lazily on a lone swing. I found myself replaying Ana's story over and over in my mind. A slight breeze brought out goosebumps on my bare arms. It was going to be a cool day, a reminder that summer was almost gone. My heart ached for Clare and Dante.

"There you are!" The familiar voice cut into my mental meanderings. "What's up with ditching me?"

"What? You haven't been showing up."

"I came by your apartment yesterday and today and you were already gone. I came over here yesterday and didn't see you anywhere. By the way, I caught that *Artero* stealing your beans back at the lot."

"Rose."

"Really—I'm not lying. Check it out for yourself."

I abandoned the swing and we rode to the lot. Sure enough, only small spindly pods dangled from the plants.

"Told ya. When I confronted him he told me that you hadn't been around and that the beans would be too big. He said he was picking them for you."

Although initially upset, I thought back to a couple of days ago. I remembered how fast the beans had been growing, and how big they already were. I thought about Arturo—I trusted him. Or at least I had. I wanted to. After Ana's story I didn't know if I could trust anyone. A part of me was even blaming her for not having told the whole story to Clare, Dante, and me, from the beginning. And my mom—obviously I couldn't trust her.

"They needed picking," I said. "They needed picking on Tuesday. And after the rain, I'm sure they were almost too big by yesterday."

"That's what *he* said." She sounded disappointed. "Have you been hanging out with him?" she asked accusatorially.

"No, of course not. I did run into him that next day … hey … where have *you* been?"

"Grounded."

"What?"

"I was grounded," she said, kicking the dirt with the toe of her sneaker. "What's the matter, Lily, never been grounded? Too goody-goody for that?"

I was not enjoying Rose's hostility. Things were confusing enough for me without having to endure her jabs. And my mom *didn't* "ground;" it wasn't in her repertoire.

"Of course I have," I lied, trying to avoid more teasing. "I was just surprised. I missed you, Rose. And I was worried. You didn't show up for three days." This seemed to calm her.

"Two days," she said. "Remember, I *did* come by yesterday. Your mom said you had already gone. She looked surprised to see me."

Shoot. Rose came by and knocked at the door? Ma knew I was gone for over an hour and not with Rose? And she never let on.

"You came to the door, Rose? I told you not to do that."

"I didn't see you and after missing two days, I thought—"

"—You thought nothing Rose, I told you to always ride around in the parking lot." It was my turn to be irritable. "Geez, Rose, you could really have gotten me into trouble. My mom likes to know who I'm with. She doesn't know about Ana."

I turned and walked back to the bikes. She chased after me.

"I'm sorry, Lily. I missed you, too. Now everything is straightened out. We're back together. Let's go back to your place. We can pretend I caught up with you yesterday and we hung out all day, if it helps. Then your mom won't be mad."

Everything is definitely not straightened out, I thought to myself. "That's a good idea, Rose, but I'd like to finish checking on my plants. I've been neglecting them lately." I was happy to see Rose, but I was also not finished sorting things out; my internal conversation begged to continue. Then again, maybe distraction was a good thing.

Back at the park, we started from the opposite end. More sensitive now to the danger, I reined Rose in, reminding her of our illegal status. I commented on how good everything looked.

"I checked it all yesterday," Rose said proudly.

"And so did I," a deep voice from behind added.

"Arturo," I said, turning and smiling.

"Hello, Lily, Rose," he said politely.

Rose grunted her greeting.

"How are you Lily? I didn't see you for some times."

"Yeah, I wasn't feeling well one day, and then I had some things to do is all."

"I hope you don't mind I picked your beans," he said. "I saved them for a day, but then my papa said we should eat them. There would be more fresh ones later."

At this, Rose's face grew dark. Fearing oncoming rudeness, I placed my hand on her shoulder and answered quickly.

"No, of course. In fact, one reason I hadn't picked them sooner was I didn't know what I would do with them. It's a secret from my mom—I'm still trying to figure out how to handle the situation."

"So, you and Rose are sneaky gardening around the city, but you don't eat the food?"

It sounded so ridiculous when he put it that way.

"Um, things just sort of happened. And some things have changed."

He nodded, as if what I said made any sense at all. We walked as we talked, eyeing the crops, sometimes chewing a little mint or basil.

"You girls gonna come see *mi jardin* soon?" he asked after awhile.

"Where do you live?" Rose asked.

"I will take you there." He looked at me as he spoke. Fortunately, Rose was looking the other way and didn't notice.

"Maybe another time, Arturo," I said. "Not today. Is it far?"

"No, not so far," he said. "Very near."

"Great!" I said. We had circled back to the playground where Rose had found me earlier. "Well, that's it. I've already checked on the rest of them. I need to get going, you two."

"Wait, what do you mean, *you two*?" Rose asked.

"Oh, Rose. Um, I have some things to do at home today."

"We're not going to Ana's?"

"Not today. I saw her yesterday. Today's not good for her."

"Oh."

She was clearly disappointed and I felt a little guilty—but there was no way I was ready to reveal everything I had just learned. And my attempt to find solace alone with my plants had clearly failed. My plan now was to do the only other thing I knew: go back, close my door, and write. I ran to my bicycle thinking Rose was on my heels, but when I stopped, was surprised to find myself alone. Looking back across the park, I spied Arturo crossing a street, heading downtown, and Rose not far from where I'd left her. She was talking on a telecommunicator. *That's weird.* I'd never seen her use one before. We had never talked about it or exchanged numbers. I would have to remember to ask her about it next time. Now that our daily routine was up in the air, other ways of communicating might come in handy.

chapter 19

I HAD LUNCH WITH MA as usual. We sat with our secrets like dead men. So this was the inheritance from my mom—the ability to pretend things were one way, when in fact they were quite the opposite.

In my room I took out my journal and for awhile simply looked at it. Today I would transcribe the story as told me by Ana. Today my journal would learn that James Gardener was still alive. That he was betrayed by someone he trusted; someone who had become a friend and partner in the Movement. I cried as I wrote, the blue lines in my notebook becoming fuzzy and thick; the drops scarring the paper as Ana's words had scarred my heart. I flew through the pages, writing furiously—the handwriting large and messy at times, and small and insignificant at others—the size and style mirroring my fluctuating emotions. When I was finished, I lay flat on my back staring up at the insipid ceiling, wondering what to do next.

I pondered the timing of Ana's disclosure: Was it because I had pushed her about contacting Clare and Dante? Wouldn't it have been better to know all of this before bringing in Rose? I had pushed that, too.

Lily, I chastised, always practical, *what's done is done, don't think about what cannot be changed. What to do* now? *What would Clare do?*

And as before, I knew the answer. Clare would pray. Some magical verse from the Bible would pop into her head and comfort her. I knew my friend well and this was how she operated. I didn't always understand it, but this is who she was and I respected her.

I picked up my journal. I would try it—sort of. I would attempt to write a prayer. I closed my eyes, striving to remember how I'd heard people pray.

Dear God, I don't know what to do. As you know, (wasn't God supposed to know everything?) my best friends, Clare and Dante, ran away because they didn't want to get caught by GRIM, and to protect their mom, and because they thought Ana was in trouble. I just found out that I am actually involved more than I thought I was. My parents were Seed Savers. And the danger is real. And now I have involved Rose. And then there is this guy Arturo—he knows about our gardening. Which Ana doesn't know. I never got to tell her about Arturo but now we aren't supposed to go to her house anymore and I still have too many questions. And now I also feel totally weird about my mom. (I was rambling; I hoped God didn't mind ramblers.) Ana said I shouldn't visit her anymore. What do I tell Rose about that? What do I do about Arturo? Should I abandon my plants? God, I don't know what to do. And God, take care of my Dad.

It was the first time I got to talk about my dad like that. It felt good, warm.

Amen, I wrote, and closed the journal. I would proofread it later.

Immediately an idea came to me—I don't know if it was from God, or just because of writing. Today was Friday, on Sunday I would go to Clare's church; maybe Ana would be there. By then I could come up with the questions I wanted to ask her.

On Saturday, Rose arrived earlier than usual. For some reason I wasn't expecting her, but after I had yelled at her she didn't dare knock at my door. It wasn't until I recognized the loud singing voice, that I looked out the window and saw Rose in our parking lot, riding in circles, making a racket. Other apartment dwellers were starting to yell at her to shut up. I rushed down the stairs to get her to stop.

"Rose, quiet! Come on up," I called as gently as I could, trying to hide my face from the other tenants but knowing it was too late.

Once in my room she noticed I was not yet dressed for going out. "Aren't we doing our rounds this morning?" she asked.

"I was going to do it later," I said. "I checked them all really well yesterday, and this late in the year they don't need as much tending."

"And Ana?"

"Didn't I tell you? She's not home this weekend."

"Oh. No, you didn't. You just said yesterday wasn't good."

"Oh, I'm sorry. No. She's busy all weekend. And I can't play tomorrow, either, just so you know. By the way, we should exchange numbers to save ourselves some trouble, don't you think? I didn't realize you had a telecom before—"

"—What makes you think I do?" she interrupted rather rudely.

"I saw you at the park talking on one when I rode away," I said. For a minute I thought she was going to deny it.

"Oh, yeah. Well, my parents are making me carry one now, since the grounding."

"You never told me what you did," I said.

"I don't want to talk about it."

"Okay … so how about exchanging numbers? That way you don't have to knock on my door and make my mother wonder what I'm up to, or make all the neighbors hate us," I said smiling, trying to lighten the conversation.

She hesitated. "Let me get back to you on that. I need to check with my folks. They might not be cool with that. This is, like, their hook in me. Not my unit for keeping up with friends."

"Oh, okay." I guessed that made sense.

"Well, I'll see you on Monday?" She asked, heading toward the door.

"Oh," I hopped off of my bed and followed her, "you don't have to run off."

"That's okay. Might as well try to get on my parents' good side by sticking around home and helping out."

With that, she said goodbye to my mother and walked out.

I took my time leaving for my afternoon plant visitation, choosing instead to stay around home for a time and help Ma with chores. She was very appreciative. It seemed like her origami business was constantly growing and that I couldn't help enough with the paper folding. In my head I kept imagining a scenario where I asked her something about my dad, but I couldn't manage to gather the courage. Sometimes I felt really angry with her and other times really close. Like we were in this thing together, you know. But every time I considered how great it was that she knew how to garden, the conversation about "gardeners" flooded back into my memory. No, things between my mom and me were embedded in stone; like a granite Buddha, there would be no change.

A slight breeze whispered through the trees. I drew a deep breath and let it out slowly. Despite all the weirdness in my life and the uncertainty of how I would proceed with my new knowledge, for some inexplicable reason I found myself hoping to run into Arturo—wanting badly to see him. Already I'd walked the length of the park, making eye contact with my lovely plant children, and dawdled in the swings, people-watching, until I felt guilty for taking up the space. Now, as I circled the fountain, I had given up. *Oh, well, I can't expect him to be here every time I'm here.*

"Where are you, Arturo?" I murmured as I headed to my bike near the maples.

And there he was. I swear he stepped right out from behind a tree, on cue, and was looking straight at me.

"Whu—?" My mouth fell open stupidly, and then I smiled without thinking. Instinctively, I wrested my face back under control. Too late; he had seen the grin and was smiling back and waving.

"Lily!" he called, as he jogged toward me. "Hey there, girl."

"Arturo, hi, how are you?" I may not be the well-intentioned-Asian-polite of my mom, but really, sometimes those good manners surfaced almost beyond my control. If I were drowning, going under, and other people were nearby, my automatic polite response system would kick in. I know this because I felt like I was drowning now, and yet here I was saying "Hi, how are you?" like right out of a textbook.

"I'm so happy I see you today, Lily. I thought I missed you." He looked around. "Where is Rose?"

"She had things to do at home."

"You are not afraid to come alone?" he asked.

"No. I don't mind at all. I used to come here alone a lot before Rose and I knew each other."

"You not know Rose for a long time?"

"No. We've only been hanging out for a few weeks."

We had reached my bike.

"Are you leaving? Lily, can you come to my house now?"

His eyes pleaded with me. I knew I shouldn't. What did I really know about him? Yet something about the despondency of my situation urged me to throw caution to the wind. I would not be my mother. I refused to bow to my fears in exchange for life in a box while others I loved were on the outside, defying the rules.

"Yes, Arturo. Yes, now is a really good time for me to visit your home."

He smiled his biggest smile, the one showing off his perfect white teeth.

"It's not far, follow me," he said as he ran away.

I climbed on my bicycle and rode, easily catching up with him and laughing as I pedaled alongside the running young man.

"What, are you gonna run all the way home?"

"Why not?" he asked. "Afraid you cannot keep up?"

Arturo jogged effortlessly through the old part of downtown. Eventually I hopped off of my bike and walked after nearly hitting a woman with a stroller. When Arturo noticed I wasn't beside him, he dashed back and walked with me.

"I thought you said it was 'very near'?"

"It is," he assured me. "We are almost there."

I rolled my eyes, causing him to laugh.

Now, through downtown and just out the other side, I noticed pocket neighborhoods of old, small houses, down short, narrow side-roads; whole residential sections I'd never noticed.

"There," he said, nodding toward the next lane. "Turn there."

We turned down a road stippled with potholes and devoid of sidewalks. At the very end of the street—it was a dead-end—Arturo stopped in front of a tiny white house with peeling paint.

"Here," he announced. "Mi castle—get it," he urged, "*mi casa, mi castle?*"

I smiled weakly at his joke, suddenly feeling insecure. What was I doing? I looked behind me and all around, studying my surroundings. Arturo missed nothing.

"It's okay, Lily," he said, his hand on my shoulder. "No one follow you. Always, I watch."

His statement startled me. *Always, I watch?*

"Please, come in." He opened the door and took my bike, pulling it inside behind me.

The room was cramped and dark, illuminated only by its diminutive windows.

"Excuse," he said, "we save electricity for other. *Abuelo!* Lily is here."

We kept walking as he called, straight through the tiny house and out the back. A wrinkled man rocked in a wicker chair under a hastily-made awning. He wore a straw hat and held an animal I thought at first was a cat, but soon realized was a pint-sized dog. He turned and watched us as we came through the door.

"Buenos tardes," he said nodding.

"Papa is still at work—"

Arturo stopped abruptly, having seen my face. My eyes had wandered from the old man to the yard. I had expected something different. The way Arturo talked about his garden I'd pictured something—well—something beautiful. This yard looked like a vacant lot filled with weeds and junk. My normal poker face failed to hide my disappointment. His eyes, too, betrayed him, registering his own disappointment in me.

"Come, Lily, look, look closely." He grabbed my hand and pulled me after him. "Do you see?"

I saw weeds. I kept looking.

"Here," he said, breaking off a flowering plant and putting it first under his nose, and then mine.

"You know?"

It was familiar; it was one of the herbs I grew, but which one?

"Cilantro," he said.

"It flowers?"

"Yes, of course. And it make seed for us to save and plant more."

I looked around, trying to spot familiar plants.

"Most of these are weeds, aren't they?" I asked.

"What is a weed? A weed is only a plant that is unwanted where it grows." He pointed to the multitude of blooming dandelions in the yard. "People ate those for hundreds of years. It's good."

I stood and stared. Could this be true? People ate weeds?

"You don't believe me? Here," he plucked a flower, a leaf. "Taste."

I took a nibble. "Bleh." Not good.

Arturo laughed. "I'm sorry, Lily. Is not so good, now. Better before the flower. But I like. And is good later, after the cold, *tambien*."

He moved through the tangled yard like a ship in a familiar harbor, pointing out vegetables I hadn't noticed and weeds he said were edible. In the stacks of tires and old sinks and toilets, vegetation of all sorts spilled out. He raised his eyebrows, nodding toward an unfamiliar and luscious green plant.

"Potatoes."

I remembered potatoes. I had read about them but had not planted any. I had no 'seed potatoes' to get started. From what I recalled, potatoes had been an important staple in countries around the world and were still grown here and used in our processed foods. They were some sort of underground crop, but not really roots. Arturo definitely had my attention now and he knew it.

"How—" I didn't know what I wanted to ask.

"You want to see?"

I nodded.

Crouching down he put his fingers in around the base of the plant, feeling in the dirt. "Ah," he said, "a nice one. *Abuelo*," he shouted back at his grandfather something in Spanish. The old man laughed.

"Good one," he told me, "big; I surprised *Abuelo* missed it. He like to 'steal' them through the summer."

Arturo grabbed my hand and put it in the dirt, onto a firm round potato, its red skin now showing; "potato," he said, "*papa* in Spanish." The way he said it gave me goosebumps. Somehow it seemed our hands were together in a treasure chest of gold coins. My heart beat fast and I felt warm all over. I wasn't sure at which moment I realized my excitement over the potato changed into an awkwardness at my proximity to Arturo.

His hand no longer covered mine, but searched for other potatoes. He was pulling them out of the ground, dusting them off.

"Go on, Lily, see if you can find."

I gathered myself together, concentrating on the garden rather than my galloping emotions.

"Try another," he said, pointing toward other potato plants I now recognized growing in old barrels and appliances.

"How?" I faltered, finding my voice at last.

"Like I showed you. Feel around the plant, how you say, soft."

"Gently?"

"Yes," he smiled, "gently."

My fingers poked down at the base of the plant. I didn't mind the dirt pressing under my nails. I moved my hand out away from the base and hit something hard. I felt out the shape of it. "I found one!" I called. I remembered the time Dante had pulled the first carrot from the ground. More buried treasure.

"Big?" Arturo asked.

I pulled my hand out and showed him the size with my fingers.

"Okay," he answered. "Take it out, Lily."

Carefully I pulled the tennis ball–sized orb out of the ground, satisfaction flooding my soul.

Arturo showed me everything in his yard. As I sat, later, sipping tea with him and his grandfather, I was amazed at how my view of his yard had changed over the course of the afternoon. What had initially looked to me like a trashed-out vacant lot, now seemed a lush and verdant garden full of life and promise.

"In California," he explained, "is different. Many people grow, there. Here, here is like a cloud cover everything. So we hide what we do. My papa say there must be a reason. He don't ... he *doesn't* want to stop, but he is afraid, a little. Something in this town is not right."

"Arturo. Your father is right." I proceeded to tell him the history of Seed Savers and GRIM and the role our town had played in it. I kept secret the part about my dad and mom, but told him about Clare and Dante and me. I didn't share Ana's identity. When I finished he let out a long slow whistle.

"Oh," he said, "this explains it."

"Yeah. Well, at least it's good to know that every place isn't quite as bad as here," I said.

"Yes," he agreed. "Hey Lily, I enjoy talking with you. I want to talk more, but I think maybe it is time for you to go?"

Time? The time! I had completely lost track of the time—my eyes searched for a clock. "What time is it?"

"Is six o'clock."

"Six o'clock! Oh, no. My mom will kill me!" I got up and ran back through the house, pulling my bike to the street. Arturo trailed after me.

"I will accompany you," he called.

"It's okay," I yelled back, already pedaling. "Thanks, see you later." I glanced back a couple of times. He ran several blocks before he fell back in exhaustion.

chapter 20

I'M NOT PROUD to say it, but I lied to my mom that night. I told her I had been at Rose's house and had gotten carried away on an old-fashioned board game and lost track of the time. I sat sullen-faced through her scolding and spent the remainder of the night in my room.

I couldn't stop thinking about Arturo. I tried to make my plan for talking with Ana the next day, but couldn't focus. Over and over, I was there under the awning, Arturo's hand grabbing mine, or down in the dirt, his hand guiding mine in search of potatoes. I wanted to write about these feelings, but didn't dare. Somehow, it embarrassed me. I'd never been the kind of girl clamoring for boys' attention. I recalled how in fifth grade some of the girls started talking about "hot" guys. Bleh. Clare and I thought it was dumb. Not that we didn't have friends who were guys. Well, collectively, anyway. Like I said before, Clare got along more handily with the male population. And yet this wasn't like with Henry or LaMonte. This, for all apparent purposes, was a crush. Me, Lily Gardener, experiencing my first crush.

It took a long time to fall asleep, but eventually ideas about what to discuss with Ana had emptied from my head into my notebook, freeing me to drift off. I awoke early, nervous about the task at hand, but refreshed and ready. My new feelings for Arturo gave me a buoyancy and energy to tackle the day.

I decided to tell Ma the truth—that I planned to attend church at St. Vincent's. I'd ridden by to check the time of the service and discovered there were two services. Not knowing which one Ana went to, I figured I'd visit both.

"Why you want to go to Catholic church?" Ma asked.

"I miss Clare and Dante," I answered. This was not a lie. "It's their church."

I knew which buttons to push with Ma. She nodded her head in understanding, her eyes moistening.

"Okay," she said. "Good."

"Um," I added, "I'm not sure when I'll be back. Church people sometimes eat together afterwards." This, of course, I totally made up based on a novel I once read.

She eyed me, not suspiciously really, more like concern.

"Lily, don't be gone all day. Maybe you take the telecom and call me if you will be very late?"

"Okay, sure, Ma." I hated using the telecom, but maybe it was a good idea. Somewhere in the back of my head I knew I entertained the notion of seeing Arturo again.

I wasn't sure how to dress for church, so decided to go with my nicest clothes—which isn't saying a lot. I rode the short distance, and parked my bike with the others.

Although intending to be early, I was surprised at the number of folks already inside. A long center aisle and two side aisles led up to a sort of stage area, behind which hung a statue-like image of a man, clearly in pain and on a cross. What was it Christians believed? It was foggy to me. I'd heard the story, but it all jumbled together in my brain—baby Jesus born in a stable … sin … a cross. *Some other time, Lily*, I told myself. *Focus.* Just then she turned—Ana! She was inside the glass-windowed room, midway up, seated on a long wooden bench. Having seen me, she turned again and waved me in. I hurried down the aisle and slid in next to her.

"Ana," I whispered.

"Shh, not now," she said, finger to her lips. "Later." She nodded her head forward and sat in silence.

My first ever church service. I liked some parts, but got really bored during others. And always, I felt out of place—when to stand, sit, kneel; the words to say when everyone spoke together. But I did feel close to Clare and Dante. The service helped me glimpse the friends I dearly missed.

Finally it ended. I followed Ana out to what she called "the foyer."

"Lily," she said. "How nice to see you. Is everything okay?"

"I need to talk to you, Ana. I have some questions."

She glanced around. "Let me see if I can find a room where we can talk. Come along."

She spoke with a man and in a few moments we walked down a hall and into a small classroom.

"Okay, Lily. Go ahead."

"Well, um," it was hard to know where to start. I looked at my hand where I'd jotted notes, the ink smeared and ugly. "If I'm not allowed to visit you anymore, what should I say to Rose? She will be expecting to ride out there."

"Yes, I've thought about that. School will be starting soon. Until then, perhaps you can convince her to ride in another direction. Or maybe for this week, tell her I've gone to visit relatives—though I'd prefer we not tell tales. I'm sorry, Lily. I regret having let it go this far."

"Is it okay for me to meet you here, if I need to?"

"Yes, Lily. This is a fine place to meet. But as always, be discreet."

I thought about the plants I had kept secret from her, but held my silence. What she didn't know wouldn't hurt her.

"Anything else?" She asked, eyebrows lifting.

I opened my mouth to speak, and then closed it, looking down at my hands. Arturo, too, would remain my secret. What possible good would it do to let her know I'd brought one more person into our dubious activities?

"Yes?"

I looked up at her. "Are you sure you won't teach me how to communicate directly with the Network using the Monitor?"

She sighed. "No, Lily. I've already gotten you kids into too much trouble. I will not jeopardize you any further. I'm sorry."

Pleading wasn't my style so I didn't ask again. After the story about my father and how his undoing had come about partly because of the Monitor, I understood why Ana felt the way she did. But I still wanted to know everything there was to know; I had to ask that one last time.

chapter 21

WE HAD CHATTED a little more, talked about the good times, imagined what Clare and Dante were up to, then hugged and said goodbye. Though cautioning me strongly to be careful, Ana urged me not to give up my desires and studies of gardening. In a low voice she told me that though it might not seem like it here, nationwide the Movement was gaining strength; that there was dissension in the government about the current food policy; funding for GRIM was on the line to be cut; and more and more dissenters like us were banding together. I left feeling hopeful.

After that I decided to peruse my lots and waysides, and of course, the park. I wasn't surprised when I felt a tap on my shoulder.

"Hi, Lily."

"Hi, Arturo."

"I saw you at church today."

"Whu—?"

"—I saw you leaving first service. You walked down a hall with your *abuela*."

"My what?"

"Your grandmother. I called to you, but you no did hear me."

"You go to St. Vincent's?" I asked.

"Sure. But I never saw you there before, Lily. I guess I must change to first service," he said, smiling.

"No, I—"

"No?" he pouted. "You don't want me in your service?"

"Arturo," I punched his arm playfully, "I don't really attend St. Vincent's … I needed to see the woman you saw me with—she's not my grandmother."

He raised his eyebrows, waiting for me to continue. I didn't feel like explaining.

"Hey, how'd you get here so fast if you were at second service?" I asked.

"The service ended twenty minutes ago— where you been?"

True, I had checked on all my other plots first. "Oh," I answered dumbly, "yeah."

"Hungry, Lily? Will you like to come to my house for lunch?"

I checked the time on my telecom. I'd love to spend the day with Arturo.

"Sure," I said. "Let me call my mom, first."

I told Ma I was eating with a friend I'd run into at church and asked if it would be okay if we spent the afternoon together. Happy I had checked in, considering my past of telecom resistance, she easily gave permission. Crazy as it sounds, I found myself humming as I rode to Arturo's, the nutty kid running along behind me the entire way.

Once again, we entered the small dark living room. And once again, Arturo shouted as he entered, "*Abuelo*, Poppy, I'm home. And I bring Lily."

Leaving my bike by the door, we passed through to the back room, better lit from the larger south-facing windows. Arturo's grandpa sat just outside, in the same chair as before; his father, in the tiny kitchen, stood over a contraption I did not recognize. Smoke from an open flame clouded the room, causing me to choke and cough.

"Hola, Lily," Arturo's father said, extending a hand, "excuse."

Arturo laughed, setting loose the butterflies in my stomach. "We like to grill our meat, but we afraid the good smell might get us in trouble, so my dad try to cook inside."

"Meat?"

"You no—you *don't* know *meat?*" he asked. "*Carne?*"

"Changing into Spanish is not going to help," I reminded him.

"*Pues*, I mean, well, you know only about plants make food?"

"Yes." I was puzzled. It was coming back now. I remembered seeing the word *meat* in some of the books. But we hadn't covered it in class with Ana. She hadn't wanted to discuss it. "Meat is like Protein, right?"

"Yes."

"Well?"

"Well, what?" he asked, fishy-like.

"Aren't you going to tell me more about meat?"

"More?"

Just then, Arturo's dad finished his cooking and bustled us outside to eat. I cannot tell you exactly what I ate, you know, the name of it, but I can tell you it was the best meal I'd ever had. We started with a type of flat round Carbo-type deal, and placed on it strips of the "grilled meat." Next we added chopped onions, cilantro, green leaves, and peppers, finishing with green and red sauces. We folded the Carbos—I can't remember what they were called—and bit in. I felt, then, that I would spend my life fighting for food freedom if only to eat such a meal again.

Peppers, by the way, come in lots of varieties, as does all food, I guess. There is what is known as "sweet" and "hot" peppers. The men would not allow me to eat the peppers they ate. Those peppers, they said, would be too "hot" for me. I couldn't understand how something uncooked could be hot, so they finally let me try. Even *Abuelo* couldn't help laughing himself into a frenzy at my resulting coughing and watery eyes. After they helped me "put out the fire", as Arturo's papa had described it, we continued stuffing ourselves with the delicious food until our tummies could hold no more, finishing with a sweet flowery tea. (But not one of them would tell me the origins of the mysterious "meat.")

Arturo and I did the dishes together, talking and laughing, but staying away from serious topics such as family, things legal and not legal, and emotions. Then Arturo excused himself and spoke to his father and grandfather in Spanish. I could tell the subject matter was serious, and Arturo was meeting with some resistance. At last he returned.

"I'm sorry for to keep you wait, Lily. I want to show you something."

He led me down some stairs into a basement, saying, "This is why we don't use the lamps upstairs."

Light from the basement flooded up as we descended. And then I saw it, tables filled with lush green plants: tomatoes and peppers, hanging full with large and colorful fruit; other plants, unknown to me, displaying small purple bells; cucumber vines snaked around gutters filled with multi-colored lettuce and vibrant herbs. Around the edges, small fans whirred.

"Is called a greenhouse. We save our electricity from other things so not be noticed consuming above normal. Is less now," he said, "because is more plants outside now, in summer." He smiled with pride.

To say I was stunned would be like saying the Grand Canyon was a nice little hole.

"But, what do you do with it all?" I asked.

"We always eat fresh," he said. "Even in winter —some. We harvest seeds. Although I did not know about your special network, we know people we trade with. Same with food. It is my grandfather's and my business. The immigrant workers, they do not like your kind of food."

"But, Arturo—"

"Yes, it is illegal, Lily. We know. Hey, I am not the one planting herbs in the public park and green beans in vacant lots!"

I blushed. He was right. Who was more likely to be caught?

"Your face change to red," he observed. "Whatsamatter, you like me?" He stepped closer, taking my hands.

I pulled away.

"Sorry, Lily. I no—I *don't* want you feel bad. Sorry."

"It's okay." I started up the stairs. "I think I should go," I said, my words trailing behind me.

"Lily, wait!" He was skipping steps, trying to catch up. "I need to talk to you about something more."

I stopped and he passed around me.

"Come on outside."

We sat on the edge of what had once been a bathtub but was now a small garden.

"Lily," he said, "you should be careful about Rose."

This caught me off guard; I was expecting something more along the lines of what had just happened between us, or perhaps being sworn to secrecy about the family business.

"I don't trust her."

"What? Why not? What are you talking about?"

"You don't know her a long time, right?"

"That's right. But you and I don't—*haven't* known each other very long."

"You been to her place?" he asked.

"No."

"What you really know about her?" he prodded. "You know her last name?"

I didn't. I didn't even know her last name. I shook my head no.

"She look at me with hate," he said. "I don't trust her."

"Arturo, I admit, she doesn't seem to like you. But that doesn't mean you can't trust her."

"Lily, on one day when you was not with her, she asked to come to my house. She barely know me and she ask me to show my house. I think this is suspicious."

"But you invited us both to your house already! You can't hold that against her."

He looked at me skeptically, disappointed-like, arms crossed defensively in front of himself.

"You be careful."

I jumped to my feet, ignoring his last remark. "Okay, so is that it? I really should be going."

A smile melted away his sternness and once again he was the sweet boy I'd so quickly grown fond of.

"Let's go," he said, his hand on my shoulder as we walked to my bike.

I arrived home around four p.m., still plenty of time to enjoy a lovely summer evening with Ma. All things considered, I was feeling pretty good. I invited Ma out for a walk, which she gladly accepted. She asked me a few obligatory questions about my day and I answered with the expected responses.

Then, to both her horror and my own, someone living inside my body asked, "How did you meet my dad?"

"Lily—"

"I'm sorry, Ma, I—"

"No, do not be sorry. You are becoming a young woman. Love will be on your mind."

Now I was really embarrassed. Was I that transparent?

She continued. "It was a different time then, Lily, a better time—and a worse time. The world changes. We go on. We adapt. I was … "

She went on talking but I missed whatever it was she said. Something about the way she spoke had distracted me. Her English—it seemed more fluent than usual—was it my imagination?

" … and he was so good to me. So patient, so kind. He believed in me and I returned his kindness and love with my own."

She turned, a smile lighting her face as I'd rarely seen. It wasn't my imagination. It seemed there was more to my mother than I knew. Not only had she kept secrets about my father, she had hidden away herself as well. A part of me wanted to cry, but seeing her beaming face as she spoke lovingly of my father, more than anything else, made me happy.

"Thanks, Ma," I said, reaching out and squeezing her hand.

I wrote in my journal for an entire hour that night. First about Ana's advice at church, then all things Arturo, and ending with my walk with Ma. I reflected on the fact that I would turn thirteen tomorrow—without Clare, yet with this new perplexing relationship with a guy. As much as I disliked putting my emotions and experiences about Arturo down on paper, I could hold it in no longer. I only hoped no one ever set eyes inside my journal; I now understood those dumb diaries with the locks and keys. Not one question was answered by writing it all down, but I felt better having done it.

After that, I practiced what I would say to Rose, wondering how she would take the news about not visiting Ana again. Rose had a short attention span; maybe it wouldn't bother her at all. I would soon find out.

But Rose didn't show up. Not in the morning. Not for lunch. And not in the afternoon. I stayed home all day, waiting. *Some way to spend my birthday*. I should have given her my number, even if she didn't want to give me hers.

Something needled me. The questions raised by Arturo lingered. Was it so strange I didn't know her last name and hadn't been to her apartment? Maybe not, but what *was strange* to my way of thinking, was the way she'd been acting lately. And now she had disappeared. And why had Arturo been so adamant about her? I'd written it off as defensiveness in response to Rose's open hostility toward him; but was there more? Did Arturo know something he wasn't sharing?

chapter 22

TUESDAY MORNING the telecom rang. "Lily," Ma called, "for you." I thought Rose had somehow gotten my number.

"Hello?"

"Lily, this is Father Williams, from St. Vincent's. It seems you left an item at church on Sunday."

"Really?" I couldn't think of what it could possibly be. "I don't think—"

"—Lily, please come as soon as possible to pick it up. I am here waiting for you."

"—but—"

The telecom clicked off.

"Ma, that was the priest at the church. He said I left something there and for me to come right away. I'm gonna ride over and get it. Keep an eye out for Rose, okay? I shouldn't be long if you can get her to wait."

"Okay, Lily, be careful."

The church doors were unlocked. When I walked in, Father Williams met me just inside.

"Come, child," he said. He led me to the same small room where Ana and I had spoken two days earlier.

"Ana?"

"Oh, Lily! Lily, are you safe?"

"What's wrong?" She looked scared, older than she had on Sunday.

"Lily, they came yesterday. GRIM agents. They checked through my house and garden. They asked me where I hid my Monitor. They yelled at me when I said I didn't own one." Her hands shook; I reached out and held them.

"They pulled out my plants: flowers, herbs, weeds—it didn't matter which. They just yanked up whatever they saw. Ignorant," she spat out the word like a bitter taste in her mouth. "I had a few things on the counter, in the fridge. They charged me $700 in fines. They said they knew I was a member of Seed Savers. That they know you children have been visiting me. I told them, yes, it was true—I was a tutor for you. They couldn't find anything to prove their Seed Savers charges. The law requires hard evidence proving I'm tied to Seed Savers or am teaching others. Hearsay or a few odd plants on my property isn't enough.

"Lily, I'm worried about you and Rose. Forgive me for summoning you here like this, dear, but I didn't know of a safe way to get in touch with you—and you needed to know. I guess all along it was me who was responsible for Clare and Dante getting into trouble ... Well, at least you and Rose weren't there having a lesson. They would have caught me red-handed. And I'm glad Rose wasn't any further involved ... How'd she take the diversion, by the way?"

As Ana rambled, a horrible feeling began creeping into my gut, spreading like an incoming tide. I was trying to put it all together; Rose never came yesterday, the same day GRIM had raided Ana's home ... For all she knew, I met with Ana for more lessons ... which meant ...

"Lily?"

"Ana, maybe kids *can* be spies."

I told Ana my fears about Rose; about Rose's recent strange behavior; the telecommunicator incident. She wasn't ready to believe Rose could be one of "the bad guys." For that matter, neither was I. It could be a coincidence.

"Rose didn't seek you out in the beginning, did she?"

"No, she didn't." I recalled how we met at the fountain that first day. How I needed to befriend her to cover my lie.

Ana's confidence in Rose made me feel better. And as we talked on, I sensed Ana calming, gaining back her inner strength. She had been rattled, yes, but she wasn't defeated. As before, Ana encouraged me to be brave. But her plea for caution was stronger than ever. I knew then my vegetables were on their own. The GRIM agents had led Ana to believe they were on Clare and Dante's trail, and once caught, they would have proof Ana had been teaching children—hard evidence against her and the larger Network. Though she doubted their threat about evidence, it caused her to worry about the children.

We hugged. I thanked her for letting me know what had happened, and she thanked me for coming.

🚲   🚲   🚲   🚲

I rode home without thinking—or maybe thinking too much. When I pulled into our complex, I couldn't remember having made any of the stops or turns; I had been on autopilot. The thoughts had swirled like a cyclone in my head as I rode. GRIM was still watching. And I hadn't noticed. Who would be interrogated next? I worried about whether I'd placed my parents in jeopardy. And I still wondered about Rose's convenient absence the day of GRIM's raid on Ana's house.

Imagine my shock when I walked into the apartment and found Rose seated at the table with my mother, talking about the approaching school year.

"Rose?"

"Hey—you're back," she said, turning to face me. "Where have you been? I mean, I know you had to go to the church, but you've been gone a long time."

"Uh—yeah." Despite Ana's trust in Rose, I treaded cautiously. There was still Arturo's strange warning to consider. "Well, I ran into somebody I knew and, you know, we talked for awhile … " Fortunately, she wasn't really paying attention. True to form, Rose had moved on.

"Hey, sorry about yesterday. Mom and me went shopping. We got a work bonus and so we got to go buy stuff.

"Wanna ride?" she asked.

"Of course." *Think fast. Think fast,* I told myself as we walked to the bikes. I got in the lead and steered Rose in a new direction. She followed without question. We circled around and arrived back home.

"Aren't we going to Ana's today?"

"No," I said. "I've decided it's too far. The days are getting shorter, and the weather is changing, I'd feel more comfortable sticking closer to home."

"Yeah, I hear ya," she agreed. "I kind of felt that way myself, but didn't want to be a stick-in-the-mud."

I turned and looked at her. "Maybe we can go to your place sometime." She didn't flinch.

"Sure. I thought you'd never ask."

You could have knocked me over with a straw.

"Oh," I replied dumbly. "Cool. Rose, what's your last name?"

"O'Connor."

She looked at me funny.

"Anything else, Sherlock?" She teased.

"Um, no. I'm good. Wanna come up for a snack?"

We dropped the bikes and headed up the stairs, my doubts about Rose as transitory as a bubble in the wind.

chapter 23

ROSE SHOWED UP at precisely nine the next morning, ready to guide me to her apartment. It wasn't far at all, and I had to wonder why we'd never gone there before. True, it was in a slightly seedier part of the neighborhood, and my mom kept a much cleaner home. Could these things have kept Rose from inviting me? Or maybe she just liked getting away from her younger sister. Lisa was, actually, quite annoying—not cool like Dante. We hung around there for awhile, but ended up scouting our regular haunts. We left the vegetables alone; I told her I had reason to be more cautious and she was okay with that.

Of course we ran into Arturo. Rose was cold, but decent. Arturo was pleasant, as usual, which amazed me, knowing how he really felt about her.

It was a bit unnerving how well he masked his emotions.

The day was hot—sweltering to be precise. After cooling off in the fountain, we hit Rose's place again for some drinks. We reminisced about Ana's ice cold tea and swore some day we would own working refrigerators.

"Lily?"

"Yeah?"

"It's been fun hanging out with you."

"Yeah," I said.

"I liked learning that stuff from Ana."

"Mm-hmm."

"D'ya think she'll be working at St. Vincent's again?"

I froze. Trap question, or true interest? "I—uh —I don't know. But she probably won't do any more garden teaching."

"Why not?"

"Don't you remember? I told you she refused to even come to tutoring those last few weeks. After she saw the agent that day, she stopped contact."

"But what about those visits we made?"

"My mistake," I said.

"*Our* mistake," she corrected. "If it *was* a mistake."

I wanted to let her know what a big mistake it had been. But a tiny part of me was still not quite certain about Rose. Arturo had planted doubt in me.

"It wasn't such a good idea," I said. "Just because neither of us has seen an agent since Clare and Dante left doesn't mean they might not be around. I should have learned my lesson before."

"You're right," she said. "I mean there is that. Their mom got arrested."

This set me back, thinking about Clare and Dante, not knowing where they were, Ana's recent disturbance fresh in mind. I looked down, silent in my descending despair.

"Lily, I hate to say this, because I've seen the way you look at him, but I don't trust that Arturo."

I looked up at her. *What?*

"I know it's unlikely that he is a GRIM agent, but what if, you know, what if he works for them. Like, if he was an *illegal*, and they cut him a deal. I mean, he could have been keeping tabs on us, right? But then I spotted him, so he had to act all nice. He could be like, twenty-three years old or something. Those foreigners often look lots younger than their actual age."

Sometimes Rose was so clueless, the fact of my Asian characteristics apparently escaping her. She kept talking.

"I'm just saying, Lily, I think if we're gonna be careful, we need to be careful all the way around."

I blinked and shook my head slightly. "What? You think Arturo might be a spy for GRIM?" I so wanted to tell her he thought the same about her, but since I still harbored a modicum of doubt, this was out of the question.

"He could be. Think about it—he suddenly just shows up watching our every move. Then when we call him on it, he's all friendly."

"He might say the same about you."

"Did he?" she asked, her voice rising.

"I said, *he might.*"

"It's not even true," she said. "First of all, we met months ago at tutoring. Second, I wasn't sneaking around watching you in the park—remember?"

She was right, of course, I knew that. This conversation was going nowhere. "Yes, Rose, I remember. Look, I think we're just spooking ourselves. At this rate we won't be trusting anybody anymore." I looked around, eyes narrowed. "Say, where is your sister?" I asked suspiciously.

We laughed together, then jumped on the bikes and headed back to my place.

The next morning I was surprised to find Arturo waiting outside my apartment building.

"Arturo!"

"Lily, hi. Let's walk."

"You really need a bike," I told him.

"So I hear. Hey, why you still going with Rose?"

Wow. Sometimes his English skills made him sound too abrupt.

"Umm, last time I checked, this was still a semi-free country."

"Lily."

"Look, Arturo. I think Rose is okay. But I'm being careful. She pointed out that maybe *you* were a spy." I laughed after I said it; it was a joke.

He gazed at me stonily. "Not funny," he said.

I didn't really want to do this. I liked Arturo. Seeing this side of him was not fun.

"Oh brother. Forget it, okay? I'm fine. But—" I was about to tell him about Ana's encounter, that there really had been GRIM agents around; I changed my mind.

"But—?"

"But I've decided to be more careful and abandon my public gardening," I said.

"Good idea," he said. "Will you be gardening with the older woman you spoke of?"

"No—I mean—school's about to start. And it's too far to go, really."

He nodded his head in understanding.

"I was wondering," I continued, "about your plant lights in the basement—"

"Shh," he placed a finger in front of his lips.

"Where do you get those?" I whispered.

"I will tell you all sometime," he said. "But not now."

"Arturo?"

"Yes?"

"Which school will you be attending?"

He hesitated.

"School starts soon," I continued, "which school is yours?" I wasn't sure of the boundary lines, or even which grade he was in.

"I don't know," he answered. His smile was weak, forced. "I guess I need to find that out."

chapter 24

EVERY DAY THAT SCHOOL DREW NEARER I felt more and more panicked. For some reason, it seemed I couldn't go back—not without Clare. It felt too final, as if she had died and I had to go on living without her; but she had not died.

I was clinging to summer like a cat on a screen door.

"Lily," Rose said—it was our last long week-end before school edged it's way back into our lives— "have you talked to Ana recently?"

"No, not really."

She was silent, unusual for Rose.

"Why?" I asked.

"Just wondered. Do you think she's okay?"

Alarms went off inside of me. Rose had a strange look on her face, like a child who's just had a potty-training set-back.

"Rose?"

"Lily, I'm sorry." She started crying. Crying! I had never seen Rose cry. She was a tough-as-nails-no-nonsense kid. Before I knew it, I was across the room, shaking her.

"What, Rose, what do you know?" I yelled.

"I didn't want to do it. Mom made me. She said we needed the money. I had no choice."

"Rose—"

"—She seemed really nice. But I wasn't fooled. I stood right up to her. But my mom—"

"—Rose, start at the beginning—tell me what you're talking about—is Ana okay?" My voice was rising, I was beginning to panic, I closed the door and turned up the music so Ma wouldn't hear.

"I don't know," she cried. "That's why I asked if you'd talked to her."

"I talked to her on Tuesday," I said. "GRIM agents visited her on Monday. What do you know?"

"She's okay?" Rose sniffed and seemed relieved.

"Why?" I asked. "What do you know about it?" I said again.

She hesitated.

"Tell me!" I screamed.

"A while back, a woman showed up at our apartment. She told my stepmom, Jenny, that I had some information she'd like to pay us for. Jenny was happy to say I'd help, even without knowing what she wanted. I wasn't home. Later, she came again when I *was* home and Jenny shoved me in front of her. It's funny; she looked kinda nice—not threatening—ya know. Small, middle-aged. But her eyes were a cold, hard blue, and her smile wasn't really there."

For the first time, Rose looked up, met my gaze.

"It was like there was a smile on the outside of her face, but it didn't go all the way through—like a mask. And when she spoke, her words said one thing, but you knew they meant exactly the opposite. She wouldn't say who she was, but based on her questions, she had all the markings of GRIM. She gave us fancy new tele-communicators. She asked lots of questions, questions about you, and Clare, and Ana, and Celia, and your mom—"

"—*My mom?*"

Rose nodded and proceeded. "She wanted me to keep doing stuff with you and said she'd be back again."

"Rose, what did you tell her?"

She hung her head, continuing her story but unable to sustain eye contact. "Well, you saw me that day in the park with the telecom. I was reporting where you were. But Lily, I couldn't do it. Everything I did, I did and said the least I could, and it was because my stepmom was making me. I told the lady that the plants you visited around town had been planted by Clare and Dante. I said I didn't know if Ana had taught you guys about gardening, and that for me personally, she had just helped with math and English. The lady didn't really believe me, I could tell by her face. She knew you and me had been to Ana's house and wanted to know what we did there. I admitted we were there and that we drank tea, but I said the tea was just from plant leaves anybody could find. And I pure-out lied about the books. 'Books?' I said, 'What books?' She asked me about seeds, too, did you have any, did Ana have any. Jenny glared at me, but I played dumb. *I liked* learning that stuff; I want to grow my own food and tea leaves. I didn't rat anybody out.

"Anyway, I had to come clean with you. I couldn't live with myself anymore. And I needed to know about Ana." She stopped. At last she looked up at me.

I felt dead; deflated. Like a slashed tire, flat on the ground, with the weight of the entire car bearing down on me. During different parts of her confession, emotions had surged through me: fear, betrayal, anger, sadness, empathy, doubt. And now everything stopped. Like the end of a fast-moving and terror-filled amusement ride, I sat there immobile, yet inwardly reeling.

"Lily?" Her eyes asked if we were still friends.

I wanted to tell her it was okay, that I understood. But it wasn't okay and I didn't understand. I had trusted her. Ana's shaken countenance looked out at me as I met Rose's penitent gaze.

"I can't, Rose, not yet."

I paused. "You should leave now." I crossed the room and opened the door. She ran out and through the apartment, hiding her tear-stained face from Ma.

I turned the volume back down and stared up at the ceiling trying to remember what it was like to have a boring and uneventful summer.

How could I have been so stupid? I no longer knew what to believe or who to trust. Maybe what Rose said was true, or maybe it was just a cover. Maybe because we'd stopped visiting Ana and my plants she had been instructed to "confess" so that I would trust her again and they could catch Ana in the act. I thought back, way back. Back at tutoring Rose had been nosey, watchful … and yet … I had grown to really like Rose. It felt true what she had told me. Her tears seemed like real tears.

I didn't know what to do. It was too much even for my journal. And school was starting in three days. In my mind's eye, I saw a cartoon pile of dynamite, the fuse burning shorter, an explosion imminent.

chapter 25

I WALKED OUT of the old brick building alone, my eighth grade schedule in hand. Health? Language Arts? Chinese? I crumpled it up and tossed it in the nearest trash can. I would not be needing this.

At home I gathered my journals and hid them in the crawl space under the apartment building. Of Ana's books, I kept three and took the rest to St. Vincent's. I didn't dare leave them at home. For some reason I viewed the church as a sort of sanctuary. Maybe because of how Father Williams had stepped in to help Ana and me. I knew the doors there were always open. I sneaked away from home, my load hidden in my backpack, and found a room filled with books. Carefully I slipped them in, distributing them throughout the shelves, among self-help and religious books. I smiled.

The seeds. I had so many seeds. When Clare had asked me to be keeper of the seeds, neither of us had known about my mother and father's role in the Movement. Now that I knew how dangerous a cache of seeds was, I couldn't put my mom in jeopardy. Yet I also couldn't take them with me. I considered throwing them in the garbage, or planting them, but that felt like a betrayal of trust. Then I thought of Arturo—his yard, the basement, the "business" he and his grandfather ran. I didn't want to explain. I rode over early that morning and took my chances, leaving a box with a note inside on his doorstep.

And then I did what Clare and Dante hadn't had the luxury of doing. I left letters for Ana (with Father Williams), Ma, and Rose, so they wouldn't worry (or report me missing).

I needed to find answers, and aside from Ana, I no longer knew who I could trust. It was up to me, Lily Gardener, to push through the darkness, like the plant inside of a seed. It was time to make my way in the world.

It was time to meet my father.

BOOK THREE

SEED SAVERS

heirloom

Coming in 2013

acknowledgments

Thanks to all the people who continue to encourage and support me in this crazy endeavor of being an author.

Special thanks to my sisters, Anita and Tracy, who I'm sure must grow weary of reading the same book over and over again. Also a big thank you to Aileen, whose creative ideas seem to know no bounds.

As always, thank you to my husband and kids.
I love you guys.

about the author

S. SMITH GREW UP ON A FARM with a tremendously large garden. She maintains that if you can't taste the soil on a carrot, it's not fresh enough. Although she now lives with her husband, children, and three cats in the city, she still manages to grow fruit and vegetables on their lot, as well as tend to three egg-laying and friendly hens. Someday, she hopes to add bees to the collection.

seedsaversseries.com

Made in the USA
San Bernardino, CA
07 September 2016